W9-BWY-057

Hide Crawford Quick

Hide Crawford Quick

Margaret Walden Froehlich

Houghton Mifflin Company
Boston
1983

Library of Congress Cataloging in Publication Data

Froehlich, Margaret Walden.
Hide Crawford quick.

Summary: Gracie and her three sisters are overjoyed when their mother has a baby boy, but the whole family finds itself sharing the burden of a terrible secret when baby Crawford comes home.
[1. Babies — Fiction. 2. Family life — Fiction.
3. Physically handicapped — Fiction] I. Title.
PZ7.F91917Hi 1983 [Fic] 82-21184
ISBN 0-395-33884-0

Printed in the United States of America

V 10 9 8 7 6 5 4 3 2 1

To the memory of Carlou

Hide Crawford Quick

I

Gracie Prayther's bedroom was lit only by the soft pink glow of the light from the upstairs hall. Her father was leaning over her bed, tugging gently on one of her braids to waken her. "Gracie . . . Gracie," he whispered.

"What?" Gracie said up from her sleep. She sat up and rubbed her eyes. Mama was sitting on the edge of the bed. "Ma, why do you have your coat on in the middle of the night?" Gracie asked, startled.

"Because we're on our way to the hospital," Mama said in an excited whisper.

"Ma!"

"Sh-sh-sh, you'll wake Lizzie and Hulene," Mama said.

"Your Mama promises us the new baby by some time in the morning," Daddy said. "We're about ready to leave."

"I'm crossing all of my fingers for a boy, Dad. See?" Gracie held up two pairs of crossed fingers on each hand. Suddenly she said, "Mama, he's going to be born right on Thanksgiving Day. November 26, 1942."

"You know it might be a baby girl," Mama said.

"Cross your fingers for a boy, too, Mama," Gracie said. She reached and took Mama's hand to maneuver her long fingers into crosses.

"Oh, Gracie," Mama said, laughing a little.

Gracie's sister Roberta came out of the bathroom. Roberta was thirteen and Gracie was twelve. They looked almost like twins — the same dark straight hair and blue eyes. Roberta's nose was a little fiercer, her figure slightly less skinny. She dashed into Gracie's room, crying, "Guess what, Gracie!"

"I know," Gracie said, bouncing with excitement; "the baby, the baby!" She felt like shouting it.

Daddy helped Mama to her feet. Then he put an arm around Gracie and one around Roberta. "You two be good," he said. "Take care of Lizzie and Hulene."

Mama said, "Promise me you won't attempt to cook that turkey. Daddy will surely be home in time to help you. Keep Huie dry if you can. Put a little cornstarch on her diaper rash; it helps. I love you both."

Roberta stood on tiptoe to hug Mama. Gracie knelt on her bed and put her arms around Mama's neck. "Bye, Mama," she said.

Mama patted Gracie's shoulder. "Now hurry under those covers before you catch your death."

After giving Mama another hasty hug, Roberta jumped into bed beside Gracie. Daddy tucked them in. "Take care of things here," he told them again. "I'll be back from Erie as soon as I welcome our baby and visit with Mama a little bit afterwards. Then the two of you can help me with the turkey. I'll call from the hospital as soon as there's any news. Keep those fingers crossed for our boy."

Mama took Daddy's arm. He picked up her suitcase from the hall and they went downstairs. Gracie heard them leave the house. She heard Daddy give a short beep of good-bye with the Plymouth's horn as he turned from the Freeport Road and onto the highway, heading for Erie.

When the car's sound had faded, Roberta kicked up her legs, letting a flood of cold air into the bed. "The baby, the baby, the b-a-b-y, baby," she chanted. Then she jerked the covers back into place and turned toward Gracie. They lay whispering until six-year-old Lizzie appeared in the doorway, just after seven o'clock.

"Where's Mama?" Lizzie asked. "Hu's pew-y. She's smelling our room all up."

"Guess what, Lizzie?" Roberta said, sitting up and hugging her knees. "Mama's gone to the hospital to get the new baby. She and Daddy left an hour or so ago."

Lizzie ran from the room, calling, "Huie! Mama's gone to get the new baby! You're going to be the old baby now!"

In a minute Lizzie was back. "Come on, Roberta or Gracie, one of you two; come change Hu."

"You," Roberta said to Gracie.

"You're the oldest," Gracie said, pulling the covers over her head.

"I have to get dressed first; I'm freezing," Roberta said. She got out of Gracie's bed and went down the hall and into her own room at the head of the steps. Her door clicked shut.

Hu was crying now. Gracie lay still for a minute, wrinkling her nose. Then she got up and tiptoed across the cold floor and into Hulene's and Lizzie's room. She leaned over the crib and said, "In a minute, Huie. Mama said to put cornstarch on you. I have to go and get it; I'll be right back."

As she went down to the pantry to get the box of cornstarch, Gracie noticed how empty the house seemed without Mama and Daddy. When she and Roberta were taking care of the little girls, only a small bit in the middle of the house seemed cozy and familiar. When Mama or Daddy was home, the house seemed safe and comfortable from the cellar to the attic. Twelve is plenty old enough to take care of a six-year-old and a one-and-a-half-year-old, Gracie thought. I know how to change diapers and put a cold cloth on bumps and get around Lizzie's fusses. I know how to cook Campbell's soup and make peanut butter sandwiches, and I could probably cook the turkey if Mama hadn't said not to. Besides, Roberta's here. I don't know why the house always seems so lonesome when Mama and Daddy are away.

In the pantry, Gracie put her hands on the counter of the cabinet and gave a little jump. Holding herself in place with one hand, she reached up for the box of cornstarch and dropped to the floor with it. Suddenly she squeezed her eyes shut: *Help the baby to be born already; help it to be a boy; help Dad to call soon.* She opened her eyes and ran through the dining room and up the stairs to diaper Hulene.

Lizzie was sitting on the edge of her bed. She had gotten one arm through the neck of her slip instead of the armhole so it was binding her tightly around the chest. "When's Mama coming home?" she asked.

"Lizzie," Gracie said, "she won't be back for a long time — eight or ten days. Come on, Hu, hold still; I don't want to jab you with a pin." Gracie glanced over at Lizzie. She was sitting forlornly with her thumb in her mouth. "Oh, eight or ten days isn't that long," she said. "Mama will be back before you know it. Want me to fix your slip? Wait a sec until I'm done with Hu."

Gracie finished with the baby and went over to Lizzie. As she pulled the slip back over her sister's head, she said, "When Dad comes home, he'll let all of us help him with the turkey. Maybe he'll do something crazy with it. The last time Mama was in the hospital, when Hu was born, we had a crazy picnic in the rain under umbrellas. It was Dad's idea. Do you remember it?"

"Yes," said Lizzie. "Where's my blue umbrella?" Before Gracie could help her to dress, Lizzie was rummaging in the closet for her umbrella.

"Lizzie, your umbrella's broken long since." Gracie had all she could do to get Lizzie out of the closet. When she had buttoned the back of her dress and was trying to brush the snarls out of her long curls, Lizzie covered the top of her head with her hands.

"Ow!" she cried. "Don't brush my hair. Mama can do it when she gets home." Lizzie ran from the room.

Roberta made pancakes for breakfast. They were irregular shapes — not nice and round like Mama's. Lizzie looked at her pancake and said, "When's Mama coming home?"

Roberta said, "Lizzie, first the baby has to get born and then Mama has to stay in the hospital for a few days resting up and then she'll be home." Roberta looked from Lizzie to Gracie. "For all we know, we could be the big sisters to a baby brother right this minute," she said.

"Is the baby going to be a boy?" Lizzie asked.

"Lizzie," Gracie said, cutting a pancake into small pieces for Hulene, "we don't know if it's going to be a boy, but we all want it to be a boy. Daddy's outnumbered around here. He wants a boy to be on his side."

"I'm on his side," Lizzie said, not eating her pancake.

"I am, too; we're all on his side. That's not what I mean," Gracie said.

"Well, you said that." Lizzie reached for more syrup.

"Lizzie, your pancake is swimming in syrup already," Roberta said. "Gracie means that Daddy would like to have a son to be proud of and to be named after him. You know how Uncle Hugh brags about Buddy and Hugh, Junior." Roberta turned to Gracie. "If our brother turns out like Buddy and Junior, we'll *give* it to him, right?"

"Lizzie, you're too little to remember, but when Hu

was born and Uncle Hugh and Aunt Nita came to see her, Uncle Hugh poked Daddy in the ribs and said, 'You ought to get yourself a boy one of these times, brother, and see how the other half lives.' "

"Daddy's not Uncle Hugh's brother; he's my daddy," Lizzie said. "I don't like the pancakes you make, Roberta."

Roberta leaned back in her chair. "Umm," she murmured, "I don't think these pancakes are so bad." She licked syrup off her forefinger and then jumped up. "You know what? This is Thanksgiving after all. How about if we redd up the house — that will make the time go fast — and then Daddy will be here before we know it and we'll help him cook the turkey. Then we'll just have a nice dinner and call it a day."

"Gracie said we might have a picnic."

"I did not. I said Daddy might think of something crazy to do with the turkey."

"That's enough," Roberta said. "Come on; I want us to do a *thorough* cleaning job. We'll start with the living room."

Roberta set Lizzie to wiping off their old piano's keys with a damp rag while she and Gracie moved as much of the furniture to the center of the room as they could. "You dust the baseboard," she told Gracie, "while I get this slipcover off the couch. Then I want you to help me shake it out outside."

As they stood on the front steps flapping the green cretonne cover, a catnip mouse flew out of it. Gracie's cat, Dionne, scooted from under a big evergreen in front of the house to claim it. Roberta went back inside and Gracie knelt for a moment to pet the cat, wondering if the baby had been born yet. On her way in to help Roberta replace the cover, she stopped in the hall and lifted the phone's receiver to her ear to make sure it was working. Daddy will call pretty soon, she said to herself.

They had a terrible time getting the slipcover back on the couch. It tore on one of the back corners. Gracie went to get a pin. She pricked her finger as she repaired the cover. "You and your redding up real good," she complained to Roberta.

"Next we'll fix the scratches on the furniture by rubbing them with a walnut," Roberta said. The walnut pieces wore out long before they had worked on all of the scratches. Roberta keeled over on her back on the rug.

"Come on," Gracie said, nudging her sister with her toe. "Don't expect me to put everything back and run the sweeper. This was your idea, you know." Roberta pretended to snore. Hulene shook all the rest of the walnuts out onto the floor. Lizzie tried to crack one of them with the hammer and struck the tip of Hu's finger. Gracie drew the baby onto her lap and kissed the hurt. She rocked back and forth with her until she stopped crying.

Roberta sat up. "What time is it? Why do you think Daddy hasn't called yet?" she asked.

"It's lunchtime," Gracie said, "and he probably hasn't called yet because there isn't any news. Why don't you go ahead and give the rest of the living room a lick and a promise and I'll go and fix lunch?"

Roberta sighed. "Well, the cleaning was *partially* thorough," she said, getting up and plugging in the black-bagged sweeper.

As Gracie fixed lunch, she named the members of the family, starting with Daddy and Mama and ending with the new baby: *Robert Charles Prayther, Bess Louisa Crawford Prayther, Roberta Sue, Grace Rose, Elizabeth Ann, Hulene Marie, and Robert Charles Prayther, Jr. (maybe). Whew!*

She made sandwiches, wishing that Roberta would hurry and finish the sweeping. The sweeper made such a racket that they'd be lucky to hear the phone when Daddy called. Once or twice she stepped out of the pantry with the peanut butter knife in her hand to look toward the phone in the hall, as though that would help her to hear it if it rang.

"Don't give me peanut butter; I don't like it. And only give me one slice of bread, not two. I want mayonnaise — just plain mayonnaise," Lizzie ordered. "Can we go on a crazy picnic for lunch?"

"No," Gracie said, "we can't. Crazy picnics are special with Daddy. Without him, they're just crazy."

After lunch Hulene took a long nap. Lizzie and Gracie and Roberta lay on the living room floor and listened to "Pepper Young's Family" and "Mary Noble, Backstage Wife" and "Stella Dallas." When "Young Widder Brown" came on, Gracie said to herself, Before this program is over, Daddy will call. I just have a feeling in my bones.

The phone didn't ring.

Roberta wanted to put off eating supper until they had heard from Daddy, even though it was getting dark outside and Hu was fussy with hunger and Lizzie was sneaking lumps of brown sugar.

"Roberta," Gracie said, "it's way too late for Dad to cook the turkey today anyway. Hu's starving. I'm going to feed her now."

"Oh, all right, have it your way," Roberta said. She jumped up and snapped the radio off. She stomped into the pantry and opened the cupboard doors. With her hands on her hips, she said, "I could fix macaroni, I could fix glorified rice with pineapple the way Mama does, I could fix beans. I could make French toast . . . hmm . . . How about French toast?"

"I don't know," Gracie said. "I don't really feel much like eating."

Roberta turned around. "Listen!" she said, "You were the one who wanted to have supper."

"I did not," Gracie said. "I said I wanted to feed Hu because she's hungry."

"Well, I'm not going to work my fingers to the bone if nobody's going to eat," Roberta said. She rolled her eyes. "Why doesn't Daddy at least call?"

They were sitting at the table eating soup when the phone rang. "I've got it!" Roberta and Gracie both cried at once. They jumped up and struggled through the pantry and dining room, each trying to keep the other from reaching the phone first.

"I'm the oldest; I get it!" Roberta squealed. She tore the phone's receiver from its cradle. "Hello!" she cried. Then she traced giant letters in the air — B-O-Y.

Gracie and Lizzie clung to one another and jumped up and down screaming, "Yay! Yay-ay! Yippee-ee!"

When Gracie let go of Lizzie and turned to hear what else Daddy had to say, Roberta had already replaced the receiver. "Hey, you hung up? I wanted to talk!" she cried.

"It wasn't Daddy," Roberta said; "it was Aunt Nita. She and Uncle Hugh are at the hospital. She said Mama was fine and the baby is a boy. Then I could hear her talking to someone in the background but I couldn't hear what they were saying. Then she came back on and said Daddy would be home pretty late."

"That's all she said? You should have let me answer. You didn't find out how much the baby weighs or who he looks like and all that? Roberta!"

"Well, Aunt Nita sounded kind of funny. Anyway, it's long distance from Erie and she probably didn't want to talk for a long time. Don't get your dander up. We can ask Daddy everything about the baby when he gets home."

Roberta and Gracie waited up, one on either end of the couch, with the radio playing to keep them company. Late in the evening Roberta poked Gracie with her foot and said, "Come on, I see you sleeping. If you can't stay awake, then go on up to bed."

Gracie's eyes flew open. "I'm not asleep! I'm wide

awake," she insisted. She turned on her side to ease her stiff back and pillowed her cheek on her hand. "I'd think Daddy would be home by now, wouldn't you?"

"I guess so," Roberta murmured, yawning.

2

Pale November light came in the window and woke Gracie. She was upstairs in her own bed. She lay still for a minute, trying to piece things together. Daddy had come home in the middle of the night and had wakened her and Roberta as they slept on the couch. They had scrambled up, demanding to know all about the baby.

Gracie sat up and hauled her pillow up behind her. She coaxed Dionne from the foot of the bed into her arms. As she rubbed her chin against the cat's soft warm fur, she remembered the way Daddy had looked when he came home last night. Once Lizzie had run off when she was about three. She had been lost all afternoon. Gracie remembered being more scared at the way Mama's face had looked than she had been about Lizzie's being gone. Daddy's face last night reminded her of the way Mama had looked that time.

Gracie must have been squeezing Dionne too tightly. The little calico cat struggled to get away. She stalked to the end of the bed and curled up with her back to Gracie. I'm being silly, Gracie thought. I was sleepy last night. His face just looked tired; that's all. The memory of Daddy's remarks when she and Roberta had asked about the baby came clear in Gracie's head: the baby was big — more than eight pounds, Daddy thought. No, he didn't think he had much hair. What hair he had was dark. Mama had taken a notion to call the baby Crawford.

Feeling uneasy, Gracie got out of bed and dressed. She went across the hall and got Hulene out of the crib. She changed and dressed her and buttoned Lizzie's buttons. Then she took them downstairs and fed them and tried to keep them quiet. Gracie guessed Hu missed Mama. She wouldn't be satisfied, no matter what. Lizzie's teasing her didn't help.

At ten-thirty, Roberta came downstairs, sleepy-looking and cross. "Why do these kids have to make so much noise?" she complained. "Did Daddy get up? Did he say Mama wanted to name the baby Crawford? I thought we had all decided to name him Robert, Junior, after Daddy. Even if it is Mama's maiden name, I don't think Crawford makes much of a first name. Hulene, stop it!" Roberta slapped Hu's hand for pulling on the toaster cord, and the baby began to cry loudly.

"Oh-h-h," Roberta said and stomped off to shut herself into the playroom beyond the kitchen to eat her toast.

Gracie gave Hu some canning jar rings and lids out of the drawer in the pantry to quiet her. She wiped the little girl's nose and combed her wispy blond hair. When Roberta came back from the playroom, Gracie asked, "Want to make Dad's breakfast and have it all set when he comes down?"

"I don't care," Roberta said.

As Gracie reached past the turkey for the bacon, she said, "Old turkey, you missed your day yesterday, but today you'll get your treatment." She found herself looking forward to helping Daddy when he rolled up his sleeves and tied on an apron to go to work in the kitchen.

Roberta and Gracie fried bacon and made scrambled eggs. Gracie went down-cellar for a jar of Mama's canned cherries and some of the grape conserve that she had put up in the fall. Daddy said he could eat grape conserve morning, noon, and night. Roberta's humor improved as they worked. Lizzie set a place for Daddy. Hulene played with his slippers under the table, putting the canning jar lids and rings into them. Lizzie discovered what she was doing and tried to make her take them out. Hulene screamed.

Just then Daddy appeared in the kitchen doorway. "Girls, do you have to let Hu cry like that?" he said. He opened the cellar door and took his jacket out of the cellar-way. He didn't offer to fish Hu out from under the table and cuddle her and let her jabber away about what was making her mad. He didn't stoop and put an arm around Lizzie and say, "Honey, Hu's little . . ." Gracie stood by the table with a slice of toast waiting for butter.

Daddy turned then and saw the breakfast. "For me?" he said. His face softened. He pulled Gracie and Roberta to him and said, "Can you save it for me? I don't think I could eat it just now. I'm afraid your Daddy's stomach is on the blink. You put it away and save it for me. I know you went to a lot of trouble. I appreciate it." His arms tightened around them. "I have to get in to Erie to Mama. I depend on you to take care of things here. I'll bring some help on the way home."

Roberta turned away to the kitchen shelf and mirror and began to undo her braids. "I thought . . . isn't Hu going to Aunt Nita's and Uncle Hugh's, Dad? You and Gracie and Lizzie and I can manage fine." Daddy left without answering. Roberta clicked her tongue and went back to fixing her hair.

Friday evening Daddy came back with a Mrs. Richards, whom they had known when they lived in Erie. Mrs. Richards and her husband had a large garden, and every Thursday afternoon in the summer they drove into town and parked their truck under a big maple that was in front of Praythers' house on Peach Street. They sold eggs and vegetables. Mrs. Richards always made a fuss over Lizzie's long curls. Once when Gracie and Roberta had been jumping rope on the sidewalk near the parked vegetable truck, Mrs. Richards had told them to stop. She said the rope was going to hit someone in the eye. Besides, she didn't think all that jumping around was good for their systems, let alone what it was doing to their shoe leather. She said she thought a quiet game of some sort up on the porch out of the sun would be sensible. The game Roberta and Gracie had thought up was to duck behind the porch railing and then jump up and make faces or stick their tongues out in the direction of the vegetable truck. They didn't think Mrs. Richards noticed, but when Mama went out to buy tomatoes and cucumbers, she complained about their behavior. Mama landed on them with a good scolding.

Gracie hadn't thought of Mrs. Richards since they had moved from Erie to the town of North East. When Daddy held the door for her and she walked into the little entry hall between the kitchen and playroom, Gracie didn't recognize her. She had been expecting Daddy to bring Aunt Nita, if he brought anyone. She could see from the puzzled look on Roberta's face that she couldn't place Mrs. Richards either. Then Lizzie came downstairs, dressed for bed. When Mrs. Richards said, "Why, is that my little Lizzie? Oh-h, what's happened to all the pretty curls?" Gracie remembered how much advice Mrs. Richards had always given Mama about dealing with Lizzie's hair.

Roberta had faded into the pantry. "Pssst," she said to Gracie, raising her eyebrows. "Why is she here?"

Gracie shrugged. Daddy told Gracie to show Mrs. Richards where things were. He told Roberta that she should sleep on the cot that pulled out from underneath Lizzie's bed and let Mrs. Richards have her room, since she had more space than Gracie did. Then he said he was about all in and that he guessed he'd go on up to bed.

Saturday dragged. It smelled like Thanksgiving because Mrs. Richards roasted the turkey. She didn't make a fancy dinner, though. She sliced the turkey at the stove and made some sandwiches.

Daddy had been gone most of the day. He came home toward suppertime with milk and some groceries.

At the table, Gracie watched him pick at his sandwich. He didn't finish it but quietly scraped it into Dionne's dish after the meal was over. Daddy always bragged about his clean plate. He would hold it up so that everyone could get a clear view — especially those who had a stewed tomato or a crust or onions pushed off to the side of their plates when supper was over. "You won't have to wash this one," he'd say, and laugh.

Tonight Daddy went upstairs right after supper. He didn't give Hu the piggy-back ride she was used to, and she started up the stairs after him, crying.

"Another time, Huie," he said from the upstairs hall.

Gracie picked Hu off the stairs and buried her face against the baby. She felt close to tears herself. She didn't remember things being this way when Hu was born. Then it seemed as though Daddy spent all of the time that Mama was gone playing with them. He had sat on the floor and played Old Maid or I Spy. He'd crawled all around the house giving Lizzie rides on his back. He'd fixed the crazy picnic.

Hulene would not stop crying. Finally Gracie took her upstairs and into her bedroom and closed the door. "Come on, Huie, don't cry. Look what Gracie has for you." Gracie went over to the card table where she had her collections arranged. She opened a wooden box and took out a seashell and held it to Hu's ear. "Hear the lake?" Hu slapped at the shell and it fell to the floor. One of its spikes broke off. "Huie," Gracie whispered, "look what you did. You broke my best shell. And it was Grandma Prayther's, too. You're naughty."

Mama always said that Gracie took after Grandma

Prayther in the collection department. That's why she had given Gracie Grandma's shells. Carefully, Gracie picked up the shell and the broken piece and replaced them in the wooden box. She picked up a sodamint bottle that held all of her baby teeth, tightened the cap, and shook the bottle for Hu. Hu reached and took it, but then she wanted the cap off. When Gracie shook her head, Hulene threw the bottle and began to yell. Gracie tried to quiet her by showing her the pictures of Campbell's kids that she had cut out of magazines, but Hu cried loudly.

Mrs. Richards opened the door. "What's all this noise? Here, here, here, here. Why, a temper like that should be conquered, not given in to." She wanted to take Hulene from Gracie.

"It's all right," Gracie said. "I can manage her; I can." She fairly pulled Hu away from Mrs. Richards, and all the while she was feeling hurt and angry because Daddy didn't come out of the bedroom and do something.

When Gracie had gotten Hu settled in her crib and had patted her to sleep, she went back to her own room and went to bed, even though it was too early. She lay for a long time thinking about how out of joint things were. Daddy seemed as far away as Mama, though he was right across the hall.

Sunday morning Gracie woke to Roberta's saying, "Psst, wake up. I want you to help me do my hair up in rags so it will be curly for school tomorrow. Come on, get up."

They shut themselves into the bathroom. Roberta dampened her long hair. Then she took a handful of long narrow strips of rag out of a box on the stand in the bathroom. Standing in front of the medicine cabinet mirror, she held one end of a rag strip just above her ear. She sorted out a small hank of hair and said to Gracie, "Okay, now just wind this hair around the strip." She frowned into the mirror as she watched Gracie struggling to wind the hair smoothly. Every time the hair slipped, Roberta clicked her tongue. Finally she said, "I suppose that will have to do. Now bind the end of the strip back up around the hair to hold it in place while the curl sets. I don't know what ails you — it looks as easy as pie when Mama does it."

Gracie said, "Well, I'm not Mama, so there. You're letting the rag slip lower and lower. You're not holding it straight — that's the whole trouble."

"My arm is practically falling off — you're so slow." Roberta raised her arm, pulling the rag higher, and supported her elbow with her other hand. Gracie continued to bind the end of the strip back up around the hair. When she tried to tie the two ends of the rag to hold the curl in place, the winding slipped and Roberta's hair uncoiled.

"I give up!" Roberta cried. "You can't do a simple thing!"

"It's not simple!" Gracie screeched. "Your hair is too bristly to hold still and your arm is too weak to hold your end of the strip. You give me a big fat pain."

The next thing they knew, Daddy was knocking on

the door and ordering them to come out. "Why are you two fighting?" he asked. His voice was hoarse and angry. His face was gray and tired.

"Sorry, Dad," they whispered. They scrabbled up the rags and bundled them back into the box. Abruptly, Daddy turned away and went back down the hall to his and Mama's room.

Roberta began to cry. Gracie went downstairs, took her jacket and hood out of the cellar-way, walked past Mrs. Richards' disapproving look, and left the house. She skirted the vineyard that lay between their house and the garden. Beyond the garden was a wooded hill. She climbed up through the cut that she had named the Big Ravine and came out into Denglers' cherry orchard at the top of the hill. She turned south, kicking through the dead cherry leaves on the ground, letting herself think of how she and her best friend, Nanny Olive Moore, had picked cherries here last summer. Soon she left the shelter of the orchard and came out onto a bluff high above Lake Erie. Her breath caught in her throat, as it always did when suddenly she could see nothing but lake and sky. She picked her way down onto a wide ledge that jutted out from the bluff. This was the place that she and Nanny Olive had discovered on their noon break from cherry-picking. They had been looking for a private place to eat their lunches. Since that day, they had come here many times to sit and watch the lake. They called it their talking spot.

Gracie stood on the ledge, the cold wind whipping her dress around her legs. She watched the gray waves crawl. Here and there they were ruffled with white.

The water made a grainy sound as it broke along the beach below. If Nanny Olive were standing beside her, she'd say: *Nanny Olive, nothing's right at our house. The worst of it is — I don't know what's the matter. Mama had the baby. She's fine. It's the boy everybody wanted. Everything should be perfect.* Gracie tightened her hood against the wind and jammed her hands into the slash pockets of her jacket. *But everything's not perfect. My father's crabby. Lizzie's bad and Roberta's impossible. Hu cries all the time. Daddy got this mean woman to come out and stay with us...* Gracie's thoughts dwindled to quiet sadness. She watched the lake for a while. Then she shivered and climbed up out of the talking spot. She hated to go home.

3

On Monday morning Lizzie said, "Gracie, I'm going the long way with Roberta and Wreath. I'm not walking with you and Nanny Olive because you two tease the Batten Woman's roosters, and I don't want to get pecked."

Gracie was just as well satisfied that Lizzie had decided not to walk the Miller Road short cut with them. She didn't feel like listening to Lizzie's chatter.

Gracie and Roberta and Lizzie attended the Miller School. It was a red brick building with all eight grades in one large room. It was about a mile from their house — "across the vineyards as the crow flies," Mama said.

There were two ways to get there: by way of Miller Road and Orchard Beach Road, or by way of Freeport Road and Concord. Roberta and her friend Wreath always went by way of Freeport and Concord, even though it was a little farther. Frank Hunter lived in that direction. Both of them were goo-goo over Frank and walked back and forth with him every day. Frank always reminded Gracie of a brand-new bar of Ivory Soap. He was sleek and blond and had baldish blue eyes. He was always winking at Roberta and Wreath.

The Miller Road was an easygoing dirt one. Gracie scuffed along, kicking a pebble ahead of her. She paused at Watermeisters' mailbox. Usually she walked Mrs. Watermeister's little girl, Burniss, to school. She was going to walk up the driveway, but Burniss' mother came out on the porch and waved her on. Burniss must be sick today.

As she approached Nanny Olive's driveway, Gracie began to feel more cheerful than she had since the night Mama left for the hospital. She met Nanny Olive down by the Moores' old sycamore and told her the news about the baby.

"Oh, Gracie, that's great! A boy!" cried Nanny Olive. She set her lunch box down and Gracie's as well. Then she grabbed Gracie's hands and they swung around in the road, toe to toe, whirling faster and faster. The silly dido seemed to sweep worry out of Gracie's head. When they came to a standstill, laughing and dizzy, Nanny Olive had some news of her own.

"We're going to Florida for Christmas — me, Dad, Mama, and Grandma Moore. The big boys are staying home. It's really a Christmas present for Grandma. She has a friend in Florida she hasn't seen in I don't know how long. They write back and forth all the time. They're friends the way you and I are — best friends."

"Wow, Florida!" Gracie said.

"I can't wait," Nanny Olive said. "Number one, I've never been out of Pennsylvania — oh, I take that back; I've been to Buffalo many's the time — but I mean I've never been in states far from Pennsylvania. Number two, I've never ridden on a train, and we're going by train."

"Lucky," Gracie said.

They walked slowly past vineyards on either side of the road. Suddenly Nanny Olive said, "You know, though, in a way I wish I wasn't going — or that you could come with me. I'm going to miss being in the program at school and I'm going to miss all the fun we could have over Christmas vacation. Remember how we ice-skated on our ditch last year?"

"You pretended to be Sonja Henie," Gracie said, laughing.

"And landed on my sitter. And we made a pact that we were going to learn to skate backward this year, or else. Oh, I wish I wasn't going to Florida."

They walked in silence past the buildings of an old winery on the left. A rooster crowed from inside a tumbledown shed. Gracie missed Nanny Olive already.

Nanny Olive sighed. "I'll bring you some seashells from Florida for your collection," she said.

"Hu broke one of my best ones the other day," Gracie said.

"That Hu," Nanny Olive said. "I wonder how she'll like the new baby."

At home that afternoon and during the rest of the week, things were not any better. Daddy was away much of the time, either at work or gone to Erie to visit Mama. Whenever Gracie saw him, he seemed tired and cross. Mrs. Richards was mean. She made them keep the radio so low that they could hardly hear "Jack Armstrong" and "Captain Midnight." For meals they had turkey soup, soup, soup, until Gracie thought they would all start to gobble.

When she was with Nanny Olive was the only time that Gracie could forget how unsatisfactory things were at home. She and Nanny Olive watched over Burniss Watermeister. They chased Earl Schuster if he tried to bother Burniss. They stared at the winery where the Batten Woman lived and threw sycamore balls into her chicken yard.

Finally the week drew to a close. Daddy took Mrs. Richards home on Sunday when he went in to Erie to pick up Mama and the new baby. It was late afternoon when the Plymouth rolled up the driveway.

"They're here! They're here!" Lizzie screeched and ran outside without her coat on. Gracie stood at the kitchen window with Hulene on her hip, watching. Daddy helped Mama out of the car. She was carrying a bundle wrapped up in the teddy bear quilt that had belonged to everyone in the family at one time or another. Mama walked very slowly.

Roberta was at the back door. As Daddy helped Mama up the step, Roberta cried, "Mama, am I glad to see you! Mama, why did we have to have that Mrs. Richards? It was awful; I couldn't stand it! I never was so relieved as when she left this morning. We could hardly breathe but what she hollered, and if I . . ."

"Roberta," Daddy said.

"We-l-l," Roberta complained.

"Roberta," Mama said, "Mrs. Richards was the best we could come up with. She's a capable woman. We ran into a trying situation with Aunt Nita and Uncle Hugh. We . . ." Mama's voice faded.

Daddy touched Mama's shoulder. Angrily he said to Roberta, "Shame on you — taking Mama to task the minute she's home. That will be enough."

Roberta hid her face against Mama's coat. Mama kissed her hair. "Now, now, there," she said. "I'm home — that's all that matters. And here's a kiss for Gracie and Hu. How big you look to Mama, Huie."

Hulene buried her face against Gracie's neck and then peeked out at Mama, not sure that she knew her.

Daddy said, "Better come in and get your things off and sit down, Bess." He shooed Lizzie and Roberta ahead of him and Mama. Gracie, carrying Hulene, followed them to the living room.

"Let's see the baby! Let us see him!" Lizzie cried. Roberta boosted her up.

"Now here, give Mama a chance to get her coat off," Daddy said. He took the baby from Mama and laid him in the buggy, which was waiting by the couch. Then he helped Mama out of her coat and went to put it away.

Mama picked up the baby and sank down on the couch. "Oh, it's good to be home," she said. The baby, still wrapped in the quilt, lay on her lap.

"Let us see him, Ma, let us see. Unwrap him."

"Sh-sh," Mama said, "he's asleep." She folded back the corner of the quilt.

"Gosh, he's little," Roberta said.

Mama's long fingers looked blue-white as she withdrew the crocheted baby cap from Crawford's head. "Let him be," she said.

"His hair is dark like mine and Roberta's and Lizzie's — not blond like Hu's," Gracie said. That was about all she could think of to say about the baby, he was shut up so tight in sleep and wrapped so well in the quilt.

Lizzie sat on the couch beside Mama and sucked her thumb. Hu struggled to get down. She seemed to have decided that she did know Mama after all. Mama placed Crawford beside her on the couch and took Hu onto her lap. Hu cuddled close and Mama leaned her head back and closed her eyes. She looked pale and worn out.

Watching the new baby sleep was not very interesting. Pretty soon Roberta and Gracie went on about their business. Roberta stood in front of the kitchen mirror, trying to make a pin curl. She had four bobby pins straddling her teeth so that her hands could be free to wind her hair. The minute she tried to take a bobby pin, her hair would slip and uncoil. Finally she spit the bobby pins into the sink.

"Oh, this consarned hair," she growled.

"Why don't you just let Mama braid it now that she's back?" Gracie said. She was sitting at the kitchen table, eating a slice of bread and butter with brown sugar on it and reading the funnies.

"Mind your own beeswax," Roberta said.

Gracie shrugged and licked brown sugar from her fingers. "The Phantom is surrounded by pygmies," she reported.

"Let me see," Roberta said, leaning over her shoulder.

At that moment, Crawford began to cry in the other room. His voice was loud and demanding.

"The baby! Come on, he's awake!" Gracie cried. Dodging out from under Roberta and almost tripping over the chair, she headed for the living room.

Lizzie's voice, rising above Crawford's crying, said, "How come this baby is broke? You should take him back, Mama, and get a different one."

"Liz-zie," Mama said, scolding.

Then Gracie was in the living room. Her mind refused to come into focus. She stared at the baby lying there in the husks of wet diaper and the teddy bear quilt. He had only one pink foot. His other leg ended just below the knee. Where, where, where? her thoughts demanded. Where's his other foot?

From beside Gracie, Roberta cried accusingly, "Mama!"

"Roberta, don't," Mama said.

"Ba-bee," said Hu.

Gracie turned and ran from the living room and up the stairs. She knelt in front of the toilet, sickness gathering. In a few minutes, she vomited.

4

The need to cry had been drumming in Gracie ever since yesterday afternoon, when she found out about Crawford. She left the house without eating any breakfast and ran back past the vineyard. By the time she reached her and Nanny Olive's secret place above the lake, a bad stitch was puckering her side. She had to lean over a little to ease it. Her breath drove in and out, drying her mouth.

In the kitchen at home, Roberta would be slamming around, getting ready for school. If Gracie had started to cry there, Roberta would have said, "Oh, for Pete's sake, Gracie." Then she would have yelled, "Mama, Gracie's bawling and she won't help with the kids."

Who knows what it would have done to Mama and Daddy if they knew she was crying? Did they cry about Crawford? How could they have kept such an awful thing a secret for all those days? Now Mama was shut up in the living room with the baby, and Daddy had been shut in the bedroom upstairs ever since yesterday afternoon.

Suddenly Gracie stooped and grabbed a stick up out of the weeds. She flung it out over the beach below, crying, "Why would anybody have to have a little baby like Crawford? Why would anybody?" Jamming her cold hands into the pockets of her brown jacket, she began to cry.

She couldn't stop. She was crazy to have come up here. She bet Roberta was having a conniption right this minute. She had to go home. Desperately, Gracie wiped her eyes and nose on her coat sleeves and then on the tail of her skirt.

When she got back down to the house, she paused by the back steps to catch her breath. Dionne came down off the kitchen windowsill. Gracie picked her up and went inside.

"Where in heck have you been, may I ask?" Roberta said. "Here I am stuck with this Lizzie who won't eat and Hulene with her diaper messed, and you have the nerve to go gallivanting off somewhere. Gracie Prayther, I could just *give* it to you." Roberta threw the dishrag on the floor in front of Gracie for emphasis.

Gracie kept her face hidden against Dionne's soft fur so that Roberta wouldn't notice that she'd been crying. Roberta opened the cellar door, took a pea jacket out of the cellar-way, and shrugged into it. Then she grabbed her book bag and lunch box off a kitchen chair and left, saying, "Thanks to you, Wreath has probably gone on to school without me."

Gracie lowered Dionne to the floor beside her dish and picked up the dishrag. She took off her jacket and hung it on the cellar doorknob.

Lizzie was sitting in front of a bowl of limp cereal, sucking her thumb. "Lizzie," Gracie said, "we have to leave pretty soon; you'd better hurry up and eat."

"No," Lizzie said around her thumb, "you can't make me. I don't have to. You're not my boss; Mama is. I'm telling." She picked up her spoon and began to poke the Post Toasties in her bowl.

Gracie lifted Hulene from the highchair. "As soon as I change Hu, we have to leave. It's late." Gracie didn't mention the worn-out patent leather shoes that Lizzie had dressed herself in instead of her school shoes.

Gracie tiptoed through the silent house and upstairs with Hulene under her arm. She took the baby into the bathroom to change her. Hu's hair looked wispier than ever and her face was chapped. Gracie longed to make her laugh with some silliness or other, but there was Crawford downstairs. And Daddy in the bedroom. Hu was too little to understand what was the matter. Gracie finished with her and took her back downstairs.

Gracie's heart struggled against going into the living room. The minute she was in there, her eyes insisted on finding Crawford, even though she didn't want to look at him.

Mama was rocking the baby. "Gracie, aren't you late?" she asked.

Gracie wasn't used to seeing Mama in a bathrobe. Mama was always one to be up and dressed and into action the first thing in the morning. She looked pale and strange. Maybe it was just because she was thin now. No, that wasn't all there was to it.

Not looking at Mama, Gracie said, "I guess it is kind of late. I changed Hu. I'll keep track of Lizzie on the way to school; don't worry. She's almost finished with her breakfast. Roberta washed the dishes before she left.

She was in a hurry to catch up with Wreath. Dionne's in and fed. I'll shut her in the playroom so she won't bother you." Words rattled out of Gracie. It seemed as though she couldn't stop herself from saying all the plain dry things there were to say.

Hulene scrambled to get down. Gracie lowered her to the floor and stooped to say to her, "You be a good girl for Mama today, Huie, you hear me? No belly-aching."

Hu squirmed free and ran to Mama, stretching her arms to be taken up. A quavering breath trailed out of Mama as she pulled Hulene up beside the new baby in her lap.

Gracie looked anxiously at Mama. It was too far across Crawford to kiss her good-bye. "Well, bye," she finally said, but her voice didn't have enough breath to it. "Bye, Mama," she said again, gruffly, and ducked out of the living room.

In the kitchen, her fingers clumsy with hurry, Gracie helped Lizzie into her coat and hood. As she arranged Lizzie's book bag strap over her head and shoulder and handed Lizzie her lunch box, she noticed Lizzie's breakfast dumped messily into Dionne's bowl.

"Liz-zie," Gracie scolded.

Lizzie said, "Well, anyways, it's Roberta's fault becount of she's the one that gave me Post Toasties and I don't like Post Toasties."

"And Dionne doesn't like them either," Gracie said, shooing the cat into the playroom.

As they crossed the yard, Gracie took Lizzie's hand and said, "Don't say, 'Don't hold my hand.' " At the corner of the Praythers' property, the Erie-Buffalo highway bisected Freeport Road. Gracie was supposed to hold Lizzie's hand until they had crossed the highway and turned, after a few hundred feet, onto Miller Road. There, Lizzie was allowed to walk by herself.

The minute they set foot on Miller Road, Lizzie pulled her hand free and said, "If you don't know it, my circulation is cut off." She shook her hand and said, "Ow, ooh, ouch." Then she ran a little way ahead and walked with her back to Gracie.

A few crows wheeled over the grape rows this morning, crying with dissatisfaction because all of the fruit was gone. It seemed to Gracie that the air was lighter and brighter-colored here than it was at home. She took a deep breath of it, but it didn't clear the heaviness she felt.

As they approached Watermeisters', Lizzie turned and said, "I suppose we have to wait for Burniss as per usual. I get sick and tired of waiting for Burniss Watermeister. Why do we always have to wait for her?"

Gracie stopped by the mailbox, paying scant attention to what Lizzie was saying. Lizzie answered her own question after a moment: "We have to wait for Burniss becount of Earl Schuster told her to say a bad word and she said it. So then you asked her mother if she wanted you to walk with Burniss and keep an eye on her, and Mrs. Watermeister said yes. So that's the reason we have to wait for her. What is Burniss anyways, a baby? She can't walk by herself becount of one little bad word." Lizzie stood with her hands on her hips looking at Gracie. Suddenly, with a smug look on her face, she said, "Wreath Robinson says Burniss should be put away."

Gracie looked up. Wreath said a lot of things about people, most of them whispered behind her hand. Gracie wondered what she would say when she found out about Crawford.

"What does 'put away' mean?" Lizzie asked, wrinkling her nose.

"It means . . . it means . . ." Gracie finished the thought in her own head. *It means there's something wrong with you and you won't do in the world, so they shut you up someplace.*

"Well, what?" Lizzie asked. "What?"

Just then Mrs. Watermeister came down the driveway, leading Burniss. "Oh, I'm sorry we're late," she said. "Burniss didn't want to go to school today."

Mrs. Watermeister didn't look old enough to have a child who was eight, Gracie thought. She looked like a girl herself, except that her shoes had little heels on them.

Lizzie pointed to a pair of silver wings, an Air Force insignia, pinned to Burniss' coat lapel. She said, "Burniss gots a new pin, doesn't she?"

"Yes," Mrs. Watermeister said, "her daddy sent her that from overseas. I told her that if she would go to school like a good girl, I would let her wear it and show it to the teacher. You be careful with it, won't you, Burniss?"

"Yes," Burniss grunted. It always seemed to Gracie that Burniss couldn't put any polish on a word.

Mrs. Watermeister stooped to kiss Burniss good-bye,

and Gracie turned her eyes away. Burniss' chin was always damp. Gracie didn't think she could kiss her if she were her child.

Gracie took Burniss' hand and moved along the road with her and Lizzie. Just around the bend was Nanny Olive's. They were so late this morning that she would be gone.

Gracie sighed. If she could just be alone with Nanny Olive up at the bluff. She might tell her about Crawford. Maybe it would ease the ache.

Gracie thought of all the times they had lingered up there talking. Now that she considered it, though, it was mostly just gab, not talk about anything really important. The two of them agreed that white oleomargarine was the nastiest stuff to ever come up the pike. Wreath Robinson's new permanent made her head look like a dandelion gone to seed. Just saying the word "brassiere" was embarrassing. Morris Knapp was cute but he was rotten.

Of course there were some things that a person shouldn't talk about. One day Gracie had been sitting at the kitchen table reading the *North East Breeze* while Mama peeled potatoes at the sink. Suddenly Gracie had cried, "Ohmigosh, Mama, it says here that Pete Moore and Jack Schuster were caught stealing spark plugs at Gordon's Feed and Fuel uptown. They were arrested. Nanny Olive never said a word to me about it. Can you beat that!"

Mama said, "Gracie, some things are private family matters. I don't expect her parents would like her discussing something like that outside the family. And don't you mention it to her either, do you hear me?"

"I won't, Mama," Gracie had promised.

If Crawford's condition was a private family matter, why hadn't Daddy at least told her and Roberta? Lizzie was such a blabbermouth and Hu was too little, but he could have told her and Roberta. Aunt Nita and Uncle Hugh must have known. They'd been at the hospital, because Aunt Nita had called from there to tell them that they had a baby brother. Gracie's mind balked at trying to imagine what Uncle Hugh must have thought or said about Crawford.

It seemed as though there weren't enough room in her head for all the thoughts and worries about Crawford. It was making her head ache. Her feet dragged.

Lizzie said, "Gracie, you and Burniss are the slowiest pokes I ever saw. It's all becount of you that we're late to school."

Gracie moved a little faster, tugging Burniss' hand. She could not turn away from her thoughts, though. Maybe Dad didn't tell us because he was so disappointed. Daddy had wanted a son. Now he had Crawford, Crawford with only one foot. No wonder he hadn't said anything about it.

Gracie blew an angry breath. But I don't want that to be the way it is, she thought. Why do I even try to figure this out?

Just then Lizzie stepped on the heel of her shoe. Gracie whirled around and cried, "Watch where you're going!"

"Crabapple," Lizzie said. Then she said, "I thought I saw Earl."

Lizzie always stuck tight to Gracie when they were passing Schusters'. Gracie glanced up at the shabby house. There wasn't a week passed but what one of the Schusters, kids or Mr., had his name in the *Breeze*. Earl was the youngest of that whole rapscallion tribe. He was more than a year older than Gracie, even though he was in the seventh grade, the same as she was.

"Lizzie, there's not a soul in sight," Gracie said.

"Well, I almost saw him. Hurry up anyways becount of I have to go to the bathroom."

As the girls reached the bottom of the hill, a rooster crowed, and another cry, like a saw striking a nail, rang out.

Lizzie hopped with alarm. "Gra-cie," she said, "don't you wish the Batten Woman and her chickens and guineas would move?"

"I guess so," Gracie said. She hardly looked at the stone building surrounded by makeshift pens.

Lizzie pulled frantically at Gracie's jacket and squealed, "Look, one of the roosters is out of its pen!"

Lizzie was more frightened of the roosters than of their owner. Nanny Olive was the one who told them that everyone called the woman the Batten Woman. "And if you think it's from *batty*, you're right," Nanny Olive said.

One afternoon when Gracie and Nanny Olive had been trying to shepherd Lizzie and Burniss home past Earl, the Batten Woman had been out throwing scratch and garbage to the chickens and guineas. She had a rusty pail in one hand and a big stick in the other.

"Hey, Lizzie," Earl had said, "you know why she carries that big stick? She carries it to lam those devils when they attack her. Those roosters can make mincemeat out of you, wanta see?" He had grabbed Lizzie by the shoulders and shoved her in the direction of the bellying chicken-wire fence. Lizzie had screamed bloody murder. The Batten Woman had hollered at them, and Earl had thumbed his nose at her. Then all of them had taken to their heels.

Now Lizzie danced beside Gracie, shrieking as the rooster standing outside the fence shook his neck ruff of iridescent green-black feathers. He split the morning with a crow. Then he lowered his head and, with his wings ajar, galloped toward them on his orange legs.

It seemed to Gracie that Lizzie was going to climb right up her back. She tore loose from Lizzie and Burniss and ran straight at the rooster, swinging her lunch box and crying, "You go peddle your papers!"

He threw himself feet first at her lunch box, raking its blue paint with his spurs and then falling in the road. Immediately, he picked himself up and pecked Gracie's ankle. She kicked him. But as suddenly as he had attacked, he lost his relish for the fight and bounced away, leaving a gaudy tail feather curling at her feet.

As Gracie turned back to Lizzie and Burniss, Lizzie blubbered, "Now my pants are wet."

"Lizzie, how could you!" Gracie exploded.

"It's your fault becount of you were in such a rush to leave that I didn't have time to go to the bathroom and it's all your fault."

5

When Gracie and Roberta had first enrolled at Miller School last year, Gracie thought it was strange to have all eight grades with kids from five to fourteen or fifteen all in one room and to have only one teacher. She was used to it now. She had laughed at Lizzie's report to Mama after her first day at school this September.

"Mama," Lizzie had said, "you should see. The toilet doesn't flush. It doesn't have any bottom to it. In faps, you can look way down."

"It sounds like an old-fashioned outdoor toilet," Mama said.

"Huh-uh, it's not outdoors. It's inside in its own little room. The pump to get a drink of water is outdoors, though. I have to take my own cup with my name on the bottom to school so I can get drinks. Today I got a drink like this." Lizzie showed Mama her cupped hands. "In faps, that's why my shoes are all wet, so don't blame me."

Roberta said, "I hope the teacher teaches you to say 'in fact,' instead of 'in faps,' Lizzie."

"Let her be," Mama had said, giving Lizzie a hug.

Mrs. Coatum was the teacher at Miller School. She was old and the same sallow color as the walls of the classroom. Gracie didn't think of Mrs. Coatum as a person. She just thought of her as a teacher in one side and out the other.

Mrs. Coatum was cross with Gracie and Lizzie and Burniss for being late to school this morning. She was even more cross when she had to send Lizzie home with her friend Agnes, who lived nearby, to borrow dry underpants and socks.

All the while Gracie was peeling Burniss' hat and coat off, Mrs. Coatum was saying, "Grace, it would be a better favor to Burniss if you would encourage her to get to school on time. Do you know it's twenty after nine?"

"Yes," Gracie said in a low voice. Two thoughts stuck in her mind: it wasn't fair about Crawford, and her ears felt so hot.

"When you get your wraps off, get the arithmetic assignment from Nanny Olive Moore and let's get down to work." Mrs. Coatum closed the door, leaving Gracie and Burniss in the dim little cloakroom, which smelled of egg sandwiches and milk and dust.

With her ears still burning, Gracie went to her seat and took from her desk a fat blue arithmetic book and her tablet and pencil and the soap eraser that she and Nanny Olive mutually owned. Then she half-turned in her seat so that Nanny Olive could point out the assignment on profit and loss. Nanny Olive asked with her eyebrows whether Gracie would like to copy the problems she'd already worked out. Gracie shook her head, turned around, and wrote *Arithmetic* on the top line of her tablet.

A row of problems staggered across Gracie's paper waiting for answers as she watched the first-graders file to the front of the room with their primers. Gracie noticed that Lizzie and Agnes had traded sweaters while they were at Agnes' house. Agnes was tucked as tight as a sausage in Lizzie's sweater. Lizzie held up Agnes' pants with one hand and her book with the other. She and Agnes settled close together on the reading bench, but Mrs. Coatum separated them, putting Leroy in between. She made Burniss sit on a little scarred green chair beside her own so that she could move her finger along on Burniss' book, following the words for her.

"Elizabeth, you may stand and read," Mrs. Coatum said.

Gracie watched as Lizzie stood up and gave Agnes' pants a hitch. Then Lizzie raised her shoulders and took a deep breath, getting ready to scurry through the story before Mrs. Coatum could stop her. Lizzie loved to read. At home, she was always begging everyone to let her read to them. Mama and Daddy were the only ones who could stand much of it.

"Read slowly, Elizabeth."

"Could I read the whole story for the kids?" Lizzie asked. "I know how to. I know all the words."

Mrs. Coatum's eyes told Lizzie to stop talking and begin.

"Okay," Lizzie said, sighing. Then she began to read.

> "Oh, oh.
> See funny baby.
> See funny, funny baby."

Lizzie stopped reading and looked up. "Mrs. Coatum, Mrs. Coatum, guess what?" she said.

Gracie felt her spine turn to a pencil of ice at the pause

in Lizzie's reading. She felt sure that what Lizzie was going to say next was "Mrs. Coatum, guess what? You should see our baby. He's funny. In faps, he's broke. One of his legs is broken off."

Earl Schuster sat in front of Gracie in the seventh-grade row. Suddenly, she drove the pointed end of her pencil into his back.

"Ow!" Earl roared. He rared up, turning to hit Gracie. She sucked in her stomach and slid over in her seat to avoid the blow. Up front, the first-graders craned to see. Earl's high-top shoes caught against the cast-iron legs of his desk and seat as he tried to lunge at Gracie. She had gotten up and was backing down the aisle. Nanny Olive put a leg across and barred Earl's way, giving Mrs. Coatum time to grasp him by his sweater.

"That will do; do you hear me?" Mrs. Coatum's order was as clean as steel.

Earl pulled loose from her, but he stopped and stood huffing in the aisle, yanking his sweater down and tucking it into his corduroy pants. "She stuck a knife in me! Prayther stuck me in the back!" Under Mrs. Coatum's cold look, Earl's head swung, and you could see he was ready to swear. Mrs. Coatum took him by the elbow and marched him to the cloakroom. As she drew the door to, her eyes behind her rimless glasses demanded silence. Gracie slid back into her seat, her legs limp.

Mrs. Coatum sat down beside Burniss. "That will do, Elizabeth. You may continue, Agnes. Stand up straight there on your own two feet."

"Two feet." The words rang in Gracie's head.

At lunchtime, Mrs. Coatum let Earl go outside, but when he chased Gracie, Roberta ran and told, and Mrs. Coatum made him come back inside. "What did I do?" he bawled. Gracie stood panting, catching her breath after the flight from Earl. It wasn't Earl's fault. It was hers. It was Lizzie's. It was Crawford's.

After Earl had gone in, the girls drifted over to the north end of the schoolhouse, where the cellar door slanted against the wall of the building. Roberta asked around for a safety pin so that she could make a tuck in the underpants Agnes had lent Lizzie. Someone gave her a pin, and Lizzie hiked up her dress, showing how much of a tuck was needed. Everyone laughed.

"Agnes is a fatty, Agnes is a fatty," Wreath chanted.

"You leave off of Agnes," Lizzie squalled.

"Hold still," Roberta told Lizzie, "or you'll get your gizzard jabbed."

After Lizzie's pants were fixed, the girls coasted to rest on the cellar door. Wreath chucked Lizzie under the chin and said, "How come you had to borrow Agnes' pants anyway, Lizzie, huh?"

Lizzie poked out her lip and said, "Shut up." Then she said, "Well, how would you like it if the Batten Woman's rooster pecked you? How would you like it, huh?"

"Lizzie, he didn't peck you," Gracie said.

"Well, in faps he almost did," Lizzie cried.

"That rooster ought to be arrested, right, Lizzie?" Nanny Olive said.

"Yes. A policeman ought to put him in jail and all

the other roosters and the guineas and the Batten Woman, too," Lizzie said, nodding vigorously.

"Oh, Lizzie," Wreath said, "you talk like Mrs. Edwards is a criminal or something. She's got a right. In fact — and the word is 'in fact,' Lizzie, not 'in faps,' you little baby — Stella Edwards has more right than any of you dummies to live on this earth. She's a healer. Yes, that's what I said, a healer."

Everyone settled more comfortably on the cellar door. Gracie lay on her back beside Nanny Olive, letting the hard blue sky overhead make her eyes water.

Wreath continued. "There was this man out to Wattsburg. I saw the house with my own two eyes. In fact, I saw the man with my own two eyes because his bed was right next to the upstairs window, the one on the left. And you know what? This man was turning to stone! He had already turned from the top of his head to his waist when I saw him. He couldn't even turn his head to look out the window. He was like this." Wreath held herself as rigid as a statue.

"For instance, if I wanted to look over my shoulder at Nanny Olive or Gracie — not that I'd want to, but say I did — I couldn't because my neck was just like rock. That's exactly how he was. Then his mother heard about Stella Edwards and that she was a healer of hopeless cases. So she had her to come out to Wattsburg to see him, to see if there was anything she could do for him, and I don't know what she did, but anyways, all of a sudden, he got so he could turn his head. Just like about this much at first . . ." Wreath took Roberta's head between her hands and turned it almost imperceptibly. Suddenly she said to Roberta, "You know, you ought to get a permanent. You would be so improved with a permanent."

Nanny Olive sat up. "Get on with it, Wreath. Get on with the story of Old Stony," she said.

"Listen, Nanny Olive Moore," Wreath snapped, "you may think this is funny, but it's not."

"I never said it was funny; I said get on with it."

Wreath turned and thumbed her nose at Nanny Olive. Then she said, "So, well, she unturned him from stone. In other words, she turned him back to flesh and blood."

"Oh, Wreath," Nanny Olive said in disgust, dropping back down beside Gracie.

"Listen," Wreath said, "my parents and I drove out past there in July, I think it was, and we drove past his house and I had this creepy feeling that I was being watched. And I looked up at the upstairs window on the left and there was this face and the head turned just like this, with the eyes following me." Wreath's head cranked slowly from shoulder to shoulder.

Nanny Olive raised her head from the cellar door and said, "Keep turning, Wreath. Turn your head all the way around and maybe you'll wring your neck." Gracie couldn't help laughing up into the sky.

"Nanny Olive, you're a nincompoop and Gracie's another," Roberta said.

Wreath stood up. "For your information, she also raised a baby up from the dead. If you think I'm going to tell about that, the way you act, you've got another think coming."

Gracie sat up and saw Burniss standing at the corner of the building. Mrs. Coatum always made Burniss miss half her recess, staying in to finish up the work she hadn't completed. "Come on, Burn," Gracie called. "Come and sit by me."

"Wreath, don't be a spoilsport; tell about the baby. I'm all ears," Nanny Olive said, hooking her braids behind her ears and wiggling them at Wreath.

"Nanny Olive, you're as feeble-minded as Burniss there, and Gracie is in the same class with both of you. Come on, Roberta, the company is getting sickening." Wreath took Roberta's hand and pulled her up off the cellar door. The two of them walked away, Wreath fiddling with Roberta's hair.

As Nanny Olive bent to help Gracie tie Burniss' shoes, she said, "Gracie, you know how fat my brother George is now? Well, when he was young, my grandma tells how sickly he always was — skinny and with earaches all the time. Well, Grandma got some kind of a tonic from Stella Edwards for him and it perked him up. Boy, did it perk him up. Once, she stopped my brother Guy's nosebleed, too, that Ma nor Grandma nor anyone could stop. He was bleeding like a stuck pig."

"You believe what Wreath told about the man turning to stone?" Gracie asked.

Nanny Olive shrugged. "Wouldn't tell her so if I did."

But Gracie still wondered about it.

6

The bell on top of the schoolhouse called them back inside at one o'clock. The safe half-hour spent on the cellar door listening to Wreath and staring at the sky had come to an end.

Gracie was no sooner settled in her seat than thoughts about Crawford and the trouble at home pounced on her again. She sat with her English workbook open on her desk and bit into her yellow pencil until her teeth felt as though they had been driven out of their beds. There isn't any such thing as a miracle, she thought. I wish there were.

Suddenly her attention was caught by Frank Hunter up at the pencil sharpener. For one thing, you weren't supposed to use the sharpener while Mrs. Coatum was hearing classes recite, and for another, Frank was winking at Roberta and Wreath, as usual. Wreath was holding her English book in front of her face and laughing behind it, and Roberta was smothering giggles in her hanky. Watching the monkeyshines going on between Frank and the girls, Gracie was distracted from her thoughts about the miracle that it would take to give Crawford two good feet.

Mrs. Coatum's pointer smacked against the chalk rail, making Gracie jump. The teacher said, "Roberta Prayther, Wreath Robinson, get yourselves up here." When they had slouched up front, Mrs. Coatum took Frank by the shoulder and maneuvered him around until the three of them were facing the classroom. She left them there while she continued the sixth-grade English lesson.

Watching Roberta standing there, shamefaced, between her friends, it seemed to Gracie that she was set aside from the other two as surely as if she had had a big black check on her forehead. Roberta was the one who had Crawford at home. She was the one who had a baby brother who was a cripple.

It was the first time the word "cripple" had come into Gracie's mind. She thought about the war veteran who hung around the corner by the barber shop uptown. His one pants leg was folded up three or four times and pinned with a safety pin. She had never really looked at his face — only at the flattened, folded pants leg pinned with a pin. That's all she could ever see.

It wasn't fair. Crawford hadn't been in a war. He was a baby. He deserved to learn how to walk. How was he going to mess in her collections the way Hu did? How was he going to climb the Big Ravine? How was he going to run down the beach to get Dad's kites when they fell out of the sky? How would he run away from the Batten Woman's roosters? For that matter, how was he going to get to school? Would someone have to drive him every day? Sometimes Dad wasn't even home with the Plymouth when they left for school. What was Crawford going to do — just sit on a cushion? Gracie wanted to jump out of her seat and shout those questions to anyone who would listen to them.

Up front, Frank was staring out the window. Roberta was staring at the place in the back of the room where the wall met the ceiling. Wreath dabbed her nose every so often with her handkerchief. Her bright red fingernails reminded Gracie of the time she had come over to visit Roberta in late summer. She and Roberta had been sitting on the bed doing their fingernails with red polish. Gracie had said, "You guys paint your moons and you're dead ducks."

Roberta had said, "Oh, for crimast sakes, Gracie."

Wreath said, "Roberta, how do you stand it? I would go cuckoo with your sisters around. Look at Lizzie." Lizzie had been sitting watching them, sucking her thumb and picking her nose. Roberta jumped up, tipping over the fingernail polish on the bedspread, and she and Wreath gave Gracie and Lizzie the bum's rush and slammed the bedroom door and shoved a chair against it.

Afterward, Mama had asked why it was that Wreath always managed to cause a commotion whenever she came over.

Roberta had sassed Mama, saying, "Hah! Wreath! It was Gracie and Lizzie who caused the commotion!" And she had burst into tears, crying, "Mama, why do I have to be saddled with these sisters who embarrass me to death in front of my respectable friends?" She had soon shifted from mad crying to the hopeless kind, and Mama had finally said, "Gracie, couldn't you and Lizzie go off and play while Wreath's here? Roberta is growing up and deserves a little privacy."

When Mama saw the spilled fingernail polish, she wasn't so eager to take Roberta's side. She said, "Roberta, I could tan your britches, and Wreath's, too."

If Gracie and Lizzie embarrassed Roberta, how must she feel about Crawford? Gracie took her pencil out of her mouth and tried to underline topic sentences in the paragraphs in the English workbook. Nanny Olive poked her, and she automatically passed their soap eraser over her shoulder. In front of her, Earl was scribbling as loud as he could to get Mrs. Coatum's goat. He was holding his pencil sideways and rubbing it across a sheet of tablet paper to sharpen it because she had taken away his latest jackknife. She walked across the room, took Earl's pencil and paper, and said, "You may stay after school and do your English." Without stopping, she walked back to the sixth-graders, dictating spelling rules as she went.

Earl slouched in his seat and rammed his feet out into the aisles on both sides of his desk. Gracie could hear angry breath hissing out of him.

The day ground to a close and Gracie welcomed escape out into the cold air. She and Nanny Olive helped Burniss cross the ditch that separated the schoolyard from the road. Lizzie trailed behind them.

"What luck that Mrs. Coatum kept Earl after," Nanny Olive said. "Now we can walk in peace."

"Yes," Gracie said and fell silent, watching her own feet move along the road.

After a moment, Nanny Olive said, "How's the baby?"

"All right."

"Does he sleep nights? My brother and sister-in-law stayed at our house for two weeks after my nephew

Brucie was born and he cried all night every night, I think. In the daytime, wouldn't you know, he slept his head off. I guess he was tired — I know I was."

Nanny Olive paused, and Gracie searched for something to say. "Crawford cries a lot."

"Well, I guess that's what you have to expect from babies." Nanny Olive flung her braids over her shoulders. "Is your father glad for a boy this time?"

"Yes," Gracie said, but as soon as she heard the word, she knew it didn't have enough truth to it to land right.

"What?" Nanny Olive asked.

"I said yes."

"I should think so, after four girls," Nanny Olive remarked. "Isn't it funny — in your family it's four girls and then a boy; in mine, it's four boys and then a girl. It's amazing that out of the ten kids in our two families, you and I turned out to be the same age. It's a miracle, isn't it? I'm glad it turned out that way." Nanny Olive hooked elbows with Gracie.

"Yes," Gracie said. Nanny Olive's mentioning the word "miracle" made Gracie's thoughts leap to the Batten Woman. If she could do something for Crawford . . .

"Oh-h," Nanny Olive gasped. Gracie looked up sharply. "You know what? I was supposed to hurry home today; I forgot. Mom's gone uptown shopping for our trip and I was supposed to help Grandma with supper. She won't let the boys help her — they drive her crazy in the kitchen with their picking. Grandma claims George ate a whole loaf of bread right before supper once. I'd better get a move on. Will you be on time tomorrow? I'll wait. So long. Bye, Burn."

Nanny Olive began to run, passing Lizzie, who had been walking ahead of them. "See you tomorrow, Lizzie."

As she watched Nanny Olive disappear, Gracie felt like throwing down her book bag and lunch box, leaving Burniss and Lizzie, and running away — slamming first one foot and then the other against the road, slicing through the afternoon, running forever. Never coming back. Never needing to find out how to live with Crawford in the family. Never needing to find out what Mama and Daddy and Roberta thought about him.

She knew what Lizzie thought: ". . . broke. You should take him back, Mama, and get a different one." As simple as that.

Bit by bit, they were getting a new set of dishes as premiums from the Jewel Tea Man. The dishes were buff-colored with rust and orange and yellow flowers. Lizzie had been the one to unwrap the new cream pitcher, and when she took it out of its cardboard cylinder, its handle was broken off. "Oh, no, Mama, look!" she had cried.

Mama had held up the broken pitcher and said, "Oh dear, that's too bad. Well, never mind. We'll put it on the shelf and I'll order a replacement the next time the Jewel Tea Man comes." As simple as that.

Here, Gracie thought. This baby won't do. We ordered a nice perfect one to cuddle and smile at and shake Johnson's Baby Powder on, and brag how cute and show off and name Robert Charles Praythe because Daddy always wanted a son named after him. Gracie groaned out loud while she waited for Burniss to catch up with her. Ahead, Lizzie was stalling because she was afraid to go past the Batten Woman's place by herself.

Gracie stopped and looked at the cold stone building, imagining that the woman who lived there could do all the strange and wonderful things that Wreath claimed she could. Gracie didn't even notice the rooster still on the outside of the chicken-wire enclosure. He was burbling along, matching step for step a hen who was inside.

"Be quiet," Lizzie whispered. "Don't even breathe." She arranged herself so that Gracie and Burniss were between her and the rooster, and she put her hand up beside her face to shield herself from seeing the rooster.

Suddenly Burniss crowed with a shattering, long drawn-out crow.

"Burniss, you dummy, I said be quiet!" Lizzie hollered.

The rooster answered the challenging call. He trailed a wing in menace and ran after the girls. Gracie towed Burniss and Lizzie as they ran up the hill. All the way Lizzie cried, "It's Burniss' fault; it's all her fault!"

Long before they reached Watermeisters' driveway, the rooster had turned back. Lizzie was still scolding Burniss as they walked up the driveway.

"Sh," Gracie said.

Mrs. Watermeister was out back washing windows. "Hi, girls — chilly work," she said as Burniss crept under her arm.

"Did you have a good day at school? Did Mrs. Coatum like your pin?"

Gracie saw the perplexed look on Burniss' face and said, "I don't think she had a chance to show the teacher."

"Well, never mind," Mrs. Watermeister said. "Can you thank your friends for walking you safely home?"

Lizzie had drifted over to a tricycle parked in an open garage. She laid her book bag down and, putting one foot on the back of the tricycle, began to push it round and round, recklessly. Mrs. Watermeister and Burniss were watching.

"Maybe your little friend would like to come over and play with you sometime," Mrs. Watermeister said to Burniss.

Lizzie stopped pushing the tricycle. "Burniss is not my friend," she said. "In faps, she teased the Batten Woman's rooster and it's a wonder we didn't get pecked."

"Liz-zie," Gracie hissed. She picked up Lizzie's book bag and, with a red face, tried to get her sister moving down the drive. She didn't know how to smooth over what Lizzie had said. All she could say was "Well, bye, see you tomorrow." She drove Lizzie ahead of her, saying in a low voice, "That was mean to say right out loud, 'Burniss is not my friend.' "

"Well, she's not."

"You didn't have to say so; you could have kept it to yourself." Lizzie broke away from Gracie and began to run.

Lizzie waited for Gracie to walk her across the highway. "That Burniss and her 'Rr-rr-rr-rr-rerr.' It would serve her right if that rooster ate her up," Lizzie said. She pulled loose from Gracie again and ran across the yard and into the house.

Dionne was waiting for Gracie. Gracie picked her up and let the little cat sandpaper her nose with her rough tongue. The smell of boiling potatoes made the kitchen right, but Mama wasn't there. Gracie turned the gas flame low under the potatoes and went upstairs.

The door to Daddy and Mama's room was still shut. She listened, trying to hear whether Daddy was in there. What if he stayed in the bedroom from now on and didn't come out to go to work? Could a baby like Crawford do that to him?

In the next room, Hu was rattling the bars of her crib. Gracie went in and picked her up. Hu smelled of wet and sleep. Gracie changed her and took her downstairs and put her in the highchair.

Mama was standing at the stove now, making lazy circles with the spoon in a pan of milk gravy. Roberta had come home and was setting the table. "Don't put any green things in the gravy, Mama," she said.

Mama said, "Parsley's good for you. Don't you remember how it says in *Peter Rabbit*, 'And then, feeling rather sick, he went to look for some parsley'?"

"Mama, I hate green things in the gravy. Mama, guess what?" Roberta said. "Wreath and I gave each other nicknames today."

"Oh?" Mama said, stirring away.

"Ree and Brr. Naturally, I'm Brr. Would you call me that please, Mama, so I get used to it?"

Gracie had gotten the silverware out of the pantry drawer. "Did Daddy go to work?" she asked. She was standing with her back to Mama on purpose, because she was afraid to get the answer from Mama's face.

Roberta said, "The name Roberta is too long."

"Yes," Mama said.

Gracie had no way of knowing whether Mama's answer meant, yes, Daddy has gone to work, or, yes, the name Roberta is too long. She left the silverware in a strew on the table and let herself out into the dusk. She foot-felt her way around the playroom end of the house. The Plymouth was not on the drive. She forced herself to open the side door of the garage. The car's smell was there, but the garage was empty. He had come out of the bedroom and gone to his job at G.E.

7

Supper was an awful meal. The minute they sat down at the table, Crawford began to cry and Mama had to get up and go to him. Afterward, when Gracie and Roberta were doing the dishes, Crawford's crying made Gracie's nerves so taut that it seemed her feet wouldn't touch the floor. Lizzie put her hands over her ears and said, "That baby breaks my eardrums."

"Play you a game of jacks," Roberta said, wiping the enamel dishpan and shoving it behind the curtain under the sink.

"Okay," Gracie said without enthusiasm. She hung the dish towel on its hook on the broom closet door and went into the dining room. She pulled open the top buffet drawer to look for the jacks.

The drawer was a catch-all. Every spring and fall at housecleaning time, Mama threatened to tip it, lock, stock, and barrel, into the trash. Just a few weeks ago when she had said that, Daddy had tried to put his arms all the way around her big waist saying, "Sacrilege, Bess. Why, how could the Praythers get on without all that flotsam and jetsam?"

Lizzie had asked, "What's flopsy and jepsy — rabbits? Can we get a rabbit, Dad?"

Mama said, "Flotsam and jetsam, Lizzie, is a lot of nothing in particular that makes a deplorable clutter in the buffet drawer."

"Well, we're getting a baby, so why can't we get a rabbit?" Lizzie insisted.

Gracie had said, "Lizzie, what you're saying doesn't make the least bit of sense." Then she'd turned to Mama and offered to clean out the buffet drawer and straighten it up.

"Hop to it," Daddy had said. "Mama'll bless you forevermore." He had made Mama come into the living room to read to him. Mama had been so heavy and weary on her feet that she didn't argue. Daddy loved to have Mama read to him. Often, after Gracie was in bed, she drifted to sleep to the rise and fall of Mama's voice in the living room. She knew Mama was on the couch and Daddy was sitting across from her in the brown chair, slippers on his feet, nursing a pipe and rubbing his hand across the evening whiskers that made his lean jaws blue-black, listening to what Mama was reading. Sometimes Gracie would get out of bed and sit at the top of the stairs so that she could hear better. Mama had a way of making a story sit up and take notice.

Gracie remembered the irritation that had descended on her while she was trying to deal with the buffet drawer. It was easy enough to put paper clips and rubber bands and string and jacks in a pile, but what did you do with stuff like a nut pick, picture wire, a valentine, Daddy's broken watch, a teaspoon from the Philadelphia Centennial, a miniature chamber pot from the World's Fair, a darning needle, two old flannels, and the remains of a broken kite?

She had had to keep interrupting Mama, calling, "Mama, do you want to keep this?" or "What do you think; shall I throw this out?"

Finally Daddy had come into the dining room and said, "Gracie, honey, we need every last bit of this stuff — the Praythers' treasure. God Himself couldn't be expected to sort out the buffet drawer. You're tired. Here, I'll help you put it all back." He took the kite's broken sticks and lined them up. Then he rolled them neatly in the kite's yellow tissue and tucked the package neatly in the front of the drawer.

As Gracie shoved the drawer shut, she said, "Whew, I didn't think it would fit."

"Remind me to fix that kite, come spring," Daddy said. "By that time, Robert, Junior, will be big enough to appreciate one of the Prayther masterpieces flying in the lake wind."

"What if he's a girl?" Gracie teased.

"She'll still appreciate it," Daddy said. "But you cross your fingers for a boy. Up to bed with you now."

"What's the holdup?" Roberta called from the kitchen. "If you don't hurry up and find the jacks, I won't play."

"I'm coming," Gracie said. She moved things aside in the drawer, searching for the spiky nest of jacks and the red ball. As she lifted the flannels, she discovered the jacks and beside them, a little pile of white envelopes bound with a rubber band. The one on top was torn in two.

These weren't here when I tried to clean out the drawer a few weeks ago . . . What in the world? Gracie slipped the torn envelope out from under the rubber band. She removed a card from it and pieced it together. It was a baby announcement with a picture of a baby as pretty as a ripe cherry on the front. Inside, on the right side, the card said:

Name	Robert Charles Prayther, Jr.
Weight	8 pounds, 9 ounces
Arrival	November 26, 1942
Proud parents	Robert and Bess Prayther

Hardly aware of what she was doing, Gracie took the card from the next envelope. Mama had not written on it at all. She had not written anyone the news about Crawford. He was a secret that only they knew about. And Daddy hadn't even wanted to tell them here at home.

*

"Gra-cee!" Roberta yelled.

Gracie gathered the prickle of jacks in her hand. She crushed the announcements into a corner of the drawer and pushed it shut. Then she flung the jacks across the kitchen linoleum. "Don't yell at me!" she yelled at Roberta.

"All right! That does it! I'm not playing," Roberta said.

In the living room, Crawford cried with colic. In the playroom, Lizzie sat in the red car she called her "boom-boom" and clanged its bell. In Erie, the kid next door had always been fighting with Lizzie over her boom-boom. "How come you gots a boy's toy, Lizzie? You're a girl. Lemme ride!" he'd roar. He and Lizzie would fight until his mother came and carried him home.

"Clang-clang-clang," the boom-boom's bell jangled in the playroom.

"All right, quitter," Gracie said to Roberta. "Since you're the one who quit, you have to pick up the jacks."

"You," said Roberta, "can wait until Kingdom Come before I so much as touch one of those jacks with my little finger." She stepped across the strewn jacks and went upstairs.

After a minute, blind with tears, Gracie stooped to pick up the jacks. Suddenly she coasted to full length on the linoleum, burying her face in her arms and crying.

It was an unsatisfying kind of crying. Not safe and free like the crying at the bluff this morning. Here, in the kitchen, she had to keep all the sounds of everybody tuned in so that she could turn off her tears before anybody noticed. When she heard Mama coming, she pulled across the floor on her elbows like a commando and went halfway under the stove.

"What in the world? What are you doing?" Mama said down onto her back.

"I'm getting a jack out from under here," Gracie said. She didn't mean to make her voice sound as cross as it did.

There was a pause, and Mama said, "Well, I don't think you need to mop the floor with your school dress."

As soon as Mama had shepherded Lizzie and Hulene through the kitchen, Gracie, with her head under the stove, wept again.

Later, when she went up to get ready for bed, Roberta called to her from the bathroom.

"What do you want?" Gracie growled at the door's crack.

"Come in here."

Gracie opened into the moist bathroom. Roberta was sitting in the tub. Gracie turned her eyes away from Roberta's little breasts. "What do you want?" she asked again.

"How about reading to me while I wash?" Roberta said. "This is getting all wet." She handed Gracie a folded *Saturday Evening Post* speckled with bath water. "There's a Babe and Little Joe story in here. Mama says it's good. She read it to Daddy. How about reading it to me while I wash?"

After a minute's hesitation, Gracie took the magazine

and settled on the toilet seat. She wiped the magazine a little with her skirt and then began to read.

Later, while Gracie was getting her pajamas on, she heard Mama say from Roberta's room, "Good night, Brr, honey."

"Mama, you remembered," Roberta said with pleasure.

Gracie tunneled under her sheet and blankets and tried to flatten Dionne under the covers so that Mama wouldn't notice her when she came to say good night. "Lie down, you goofy cat," she whispered, "lie down. Mind me."

Last August, the Praythers had been visiting Uncle Hugh, Daddy's brother. Uncle Hugh had a farm out toward Meadville. Gracie and Roberta and Lizzie had been outside with Buddy and Hugh, Junior, their cousins.

Uncle Hugh had a collie, King, that was just as loud-mouthed as he was. That afternoon, King had discovered an abandoned kitten under the porch steps. He dug out turf with his claws, yelping wildly.

"Sic 'em, sic 'em!" Junior and Buddy goaded King. Suddenly the kitten ran from the spidered safety under the steps. King grabbed it and ran, flinging it into the air and letting it drop. When he charged back to scrape it from the grass, Gracie hit the dog with a baseball bat. He let out a shrill cry. The kitten lay on the grass like rain-wet dandelion fluff. Gracie gentled it into her cupped hands, yelling at the boys, "Your dumb-headed dog is a murderer!"

When she got into the kitchen, where Uncle Hugh and Aunt Nita and Daddy and Mama were talking, Gracie saw the hole King had torn in the kitten's side.

"Ooh, Gracie," Mama said.

Daddy reached his hands under hers as though the kitten were too heavy to hold. Gracie's eyes sought the wound again in horror.

Aunt Nita gave a little squeal and cried, "Get it out of here!"

Uncle Hugh held the door open. "Well, there's one cat that won't make the riffle. Come on, Gracie, get it out of here; go dump it under a bush."

Gracie had never understood how Daddy could love Uncle Hugh, big and bronze and loud. Daddy set store by whatever Uncle Hugh said or did. He'd even named Hulene after him. That afternoon, though, he hadn't listened to Uncle Hugh. He'd gone outside with Gracie, following her to the Plymouth. Wordlessly, he opened the car door for her. She had sat on the back seat with the kitten in her lap, offering it what comfort she could by smoothing its paw with a finger while Daddy rounded up the rest of the family and they went home.

The kitten lived. Gracie named it Dionne after the quintuplet babies in the Karo syrup advertisement in the *Saturday Evening Post*. It was a girl cat and it was the fifth girl in their family — fifth after her and Roberta and Lizzie and Hulene.

"Now lie still," she whispered to Dionne, "before Mama makes you get out of here." Gracie arranged herself with her hands above the covers and her feet feeling Dionne's warm softness at the bottom of the bed. Mama came in and bent to kiss her.

"Mama?" she said. A car hummed out on Freeport Road. Its headlights rode up the bedroom walls.

"Yes?"

"Mama, did Mrs. Richards know what was the matter with Crawford?"

There was a long pause and then Mama said, "No."

In the darkened room, Gracie knelt up on the bed and put her arms around Mama's neck. "I feel sorry for Crawford," she said at last in a choked whisper.

"Don't, Gracie, don't," Mama said, patting and patting her. "Don't be sorry for Crawford. He's a lovely baby. We'll treat him just like any other baby — like you or Roberta or Lizzie or Hu. Why, he's growing already. Before long, he'll blossom — you'll see."

Gracie could hear Crawford begin to fuss in Mama and Daddy's room. She wanted to cry out, Mama! He's not like the rest of us. How can you say that! He only has one foot!

"There, he's crying," Mama said. "Tuck down, now. I must go to him."

Abruptly, Gracie turned away. She lay down with her back to Mama and tugged the covers up over herself. Questions filled her mind: What about the announcements in the buffet drawer? Why did you decide to name him Crawford instead of Robert? What does Daddy think? Why didn't he tell us?

"Gracie?" Mama's hand rested on her shoulder for an instant. Then Crawford's loud crying pulled her away.

Gracie buried her face in the pillow and wept. I know what Dad thinks, I know, I know, I know. He didn't say anything because he couldn't.

At last Gracie stopped crying. Crawford's here. Maybe Daddy doesn't want him. Maybe he wouldn't let Mama name him after him. Gracie felt more frightened and confused than ever.

8

As Gracie walked along Miller Road beside Lizzie the next morning, she was thinking that it would have been better if their family had stopped after Hulene. There was no law that said families had to have boys. If Uncle Hugh wasn't such a brag about what All-American boys Buddy and Hugh, Junior, were. If he didn't say things like, "Buddy, show Uncle Robert how you can belt that ball out into the pasture," or "Robert, take a look at the shoulders Junior's getting on him. Ought to get yourself a boy, brother."

Gracie sighed and Lizzie looked up sharply. "I didn't do anything," she said.

"I didn't say you did," Gracie said.

"Well, you sounded like you said it," Lizzie insisted.

"Lizzie, how can I sound like I'm saying something when I'm not even talking? Answer me that."

"I don't have to answer you if I don't want to. And you can't make me."

"Want to bet?"

"Yes," Lizzie said, "fifty cents. And you don't know

where my hanky with fifty cents in it is, so ha, ha, ha." Lizzie skipped a few steps ahead. Secretly, Gracie was glad for the silly mixed-up argument. It kept her from thinking about Daddy and Crawford.

Burniss wasn't waiting by the mailbox. "You stay right here and wait," Gracie told Lizzie and started up the drive. She dreaded facing Mrs. Watermeister after what Lizzie had said about not being Burniss' friend. She felt angry with Lizzie. She even felt angry with Burniss, as though it were her fault that she was so slow that no one liked her. Then she thought about Crawford. Kids were not going to be his friend, either, because there was something the matter with him. His own family didn't even like him.

Mrs. Watermeister had just come out of the house, with a sweater thrown over her shoulders. "I was going to run down," she said. "Burniss doesn't want to go to school again. She looks droopy — maybe it's a cold coming on. I guess I'll keep her home. I'd appreciate it if you could ask for her books and drop them off so I can help her catch up."

"Okay," Gracie said. "Sorry Burniss is sick." She turned and ran down the drive.

Lizzie was standing where Gracie had left her. "You bet the Batten Woman's rooster is still loose?" Lizzie asked.

Gracie said, "I'm not betting with you in case I win and you refuse to pay off. You said you wouldn't tell me where your fifty cents is."

"Gra-ceee," Lizzie said in irritation. She stamped her foot. "Tell me if you think the rooster is loose or not."

"I don't think it's loose."

"You're just saying that."

"You wanted me to say it, so I said it."

They were still arguing when they came to Nanny Olive's. She came running down the drive. "Oh, I thought I'd missed you," she said. "Yesterday you were late; today I am. My grandmother is helping me make something for your baby brother. She got me started last night and I worked on it after she went to bed and wouldn't you know, I made a mistake. She was helping me to pull it out this morning and get it right. I lost track of the time."

A rooster crowed and Lizzie jumped to Gracie's side and held on to her, jumping with alarm.

"Lizzie, stop it," Gracie said.

Nanny Olive said, "Come on, Lizzie, we'll run. Take my hand and take Gracie's. Here, I'll carry your lunch box for you."

Nanny Olive took Lizzie's lunch box, but Lizzie wailed, "I have Agnes' pants to carry, too." She held up a little brown bag. "I'm returning them to her."

"Let Gracie carry them," Nanny Olive said. She handed the brown bag to Gracie.

The girls took Lizzie's hands and began to run. The rooster was perched on the fence, waiting. His yellow eyes glittered. Lizzie screamed as Nanny Olive and Gracie dragged her faster than her feet would go. Suddenly Gracie cried, "No! I dropped Agnes' pants!" She let go of Lizzie's hand and raced back for the brown bag lying in the road. The rooster sailed off the fence. Gracie retrieved the bag, but as she was turning, she stumbled and fell. Nanny Olive left Lizzie screaming and rushed at the rooster. He bounced across the roadside ditch, flapped his wings, and gave a crow of victory.

"Ooh, Gracie," Nanny Olive said, looking at Gracie's bloody knees in dismay.

By midmorning, the pain in her knees had quieted. In spite of Earl's almost constant jarring of her desk, which was attached to his seat, Gracie was pleased with the appearance of her handwriting paper. She sat reading the poem by Walt Whitman that she had copied out of her reader. Her eyes caught on two of the lines:

> But O heart! heart! heart!
>   O the bleeding drops of red . . .

Her own heart picked up the rhythm of the words, beating them out like a tune it knew. No matter what she was doing, thoughts of Crawford followed her. Was it herself she felt sorry for? Or Daddy, because he wanted a son? Or Mama, having to take care of Crawford? Or Roberta, who cared a lot about what Wreath thought?

Suddenly it occurred to Gracie that Crawford didn't even realize what he was like yet. She couldn't stand the thought. Her knee jerked, banging against the bottom of her desk and making her wince.

Just then, Earl turned around, grabbed her pencil, and slashed the word SHIT across her handwriting paper. He broke her pencil in two and threw the pieces on the floor. As she bent to pick up the broken pencil, she guessed that now Earl was even with her for jabbing him in the back yesterday. She sat up and sighed as she tore up her handwriting paper.

9

The bell marked the end of the noontime recess. Gracie was in her seat when Roberta came into the room with her eyes squeezed shut and a foolish look on her face. Wreath had brought her hair curler to school, and during recess she and Roberta had sat on the cellar door while Wreath had manufactured a whole covey of curls on top of Roberta's head.

"Woo-woo," Frank called and gave a wolf whistle when he saw Roberta.

She put her folded arms over her head for shelter and slid into her seat. "Frankie, you stop that," she squealed.

Mrs. Coatum moved across the front of the room. Gracie could see that Roberta was trying not to look at her. By and by, under Mrs. Coatum's disapproving stare, Roberta's fingers sneaked up to release the bobby pins that held her ridiculous hairdo together. Satisfied, Mrs. Coatum moved to the other side of the room to hear the third-graders' geography lesson.

Gracie slouched in her seat with her geography book propped up on the desk in front of her. From behind, she felt Nanny Olive fish her braids from behind her back and stretch them across her desk. Sun leaned through the windows. The room smelled of chalk dust and Vicks, lying winter-wise under flannel on somebody's chest. Gracie tried to read the geography lesson, but Crawford dragged at her thoughts. Nanny Olive was still fooling with her braids. At last she lowered them back over Gracie's shoulders with a whispered "Look." One of the braids still bore the green plaid ribbon that Gracie had tied on it that morning; the other one was decorated with Nanny Olive's yellow ribbon. Gracie turned to look at Nanny Olive. Her braids, too, sported one green plaid ribbon and one yellow one. She winked at Gracie, and Gracie winked back.

A while later Mrs. Coatum moved to their side of the room for geography. She called on Gracie first. "Tell us what you've found out about the customs of the Bedouins."

Slowly, Gracie rose. Her eyes were racing like mice over the words in the book on her desk. She couldn't find the place. "The Bedouins . . . well . . ."

"It looks to me as though you're not prepared," Mrs. Coatum said. Her faded eyes were demanding.

"Well, I was reading it, but I can't remember," Gracie said lamely.

"Sit down, Grace." Gracie slid into her seat, her cheeks burning.

"Roberta. We'll see if you have applied yourself."

Roberta stood. "The habits of the Bedouins — or I mean, the customs?" she asked.

"Wasn't that the assignment for this afternoon?"

"Yes. Well, they have this drink and it's called . . . lemme see . . ." Roberta's head bent over the book spread on her desk. Her hair fell in her eyes, and she had to gather it up and hold it back with her hands. Mrs. Coatum's impatience built.

"Oh, here it is, right here. I've got it. It was called kumiss." But Roberta pronounced the word so that it sounded like "cow mess." The seventh- and eighth-graders roared with laughter. Frank gave another wolf whistle. Roberta started to laugh, and Gracie could see that she couldn't stop herself. Gracie laughed, too. She laughed until tears ran down her cheeks. She laughed until she thought she'd wet her pants. For the whole time, she didn't even think once about Crawford.

After school, Gracie and Nanny Olive were in the cloakroom, putting on their coats.

"Like the new style, Wreath?" Nanny Olive asked. She and Gracie hung on one another's necks like a pair of drunks and wagged the ends of their braids tied with mismatched ribbons. "We've sworn to be blood brothers until death us do part and this shall be the sign," Nanny Olive intoned. Then she and Gracie rushed at Wreath, bedeviling her with the ends of their braids and laughing.

"How about if we strangle anyone who owns a curler?" Nanny Olive said. She and Gracie tripped over one another and fell in a heap, laughing.

Wreath drew back in disgust. "Nincompoops," she said, putting on her coat.

While they were sitting on the floor, Nanny Olive and Gracie tied themselves together with their braids. They staggered to their feet as Roberta and Frank came into the cloakroom. Frank tried to sidestep them. Roberta tried to break between them. "Woe to anyone who tries to separate blood brothers," Nanny Olive said.

Roberta tried to kill them with a look without Frank's noticing. Gracie decided not to let her get away with it. "Aren't you afraid your face will freeze that way?" she asked. Then she mimicked the face Roberta had made. She and Nanny Olive laughed uproariously. Frank's face was pinker than usual as he and Wreath went out the door together, leaving Roberta to tag behind.

Before she followed, Roberta aimed a kick at Gracie and hissed, "You are so embarrassing." Gracie and Nanny Olive fell against one another, overcome. Suddenly, Mrs. Coatum appeared in the doorway and the fun evaporated.

Gracie and Nanny Olive struggled to their feet. Nanny Olive changed her tune. "Gosh, I'd better get on home," she said quietly. "We're leaving on the twentieth. That gives me only twelve days to finish the present for your baby. At the rate I'm going . . ." Nanny Olive's face was red. Gracie knew hers was, too, as they worked desperately to untie their braids.

"So long," Gracie whispered when at last she and Nanny Olive had gotten themselves separated. Nanny Olive left, and Mrs. Coatum turned back into the classroom. Lizzie was still dillydallying with Agnes Churchill.

"I'm leaving, Lizzie," Gracie said. She left Lizzie stirring in her book bag and pushed through the door. She crossed the playground and started slowly down the road.

It was some time before Gracie was aware of Lizzie and Agnes chirping along behind her. She turned and said, "Agnes, you'd better go on home."

Agnes and Lizzie had queer looks on their faces. They giggled at one another. Gracie said, "Come on now, you two. Agnes' mother is going to get after her for being late. Go on, Agnes." All the time, Gracie was taking slow steps backward.

Lizzie said, "Agnes is coming over our house. Her mother said she could. In faps, she said so when I took Agnes' pants back to her this morning. I said, 'Mrs. Churchill, would it be okay if Agnes comes over my house to play this afternoon; my father can bring her home.' And Mrs. Churchill said it was okay." Agnes and Lizzie giggled at each other. "If you don't believe me, you can ask Agnes' mother, so ha, ha, ha," Lizzie said.

Agnes can't come over, Gracie thought fiercely. She can't go running through the house to stand by the buggy and stare. Lizzie and Agnes saw the look on Gracie's face, and their giggles withered.

"But I asked her mother," Lizzie whined.

"Yeah, she asked; I heard her with my own ears," Agnes said. "My mother said it was okay. I heard her with my own ears, huh, Lizzie?"

"How'll you get home?" Gracie challenged.

"Lizzie said her father can bring me."

"Well, he can't."

"Gracie, he can so; he can drive Agnes home."

"He can't." Gracie's voice was taut. "He's on the evening shift. He won't be home. The car will be gone.

Agnes will have no way to get home. She can't come over." Gracie knew she had lied to Lizzie. She knew Daddy wasn't on the evening shift tonight.

Soon, Agnes backed away reluctantly. "Bye, Agnes," Lizzie said.

"Don't invite Agnes over. Don't invite anybody over," Gracie hissed as she and Lizzie walked on down the road.

"I can if I . . ." Lizzie saw the look on Gracie's face. She ran with her lunch box and book bag banging against her side.

Gracie followed slowly. Inside, she felt as stiff and black as licorice, and it frightened her. They were in sight of the Batten Woman's when she remembered that she had promised to bring Burniss' books.

"Lizzie," she called. "Wait there for me; I forgot something."

Instead of waiting, Lizzie followed her all the way back to school, crying, "Wait up! Wait up!" Gracie left her standing on the steps and went inside.

Mrs. Coatum was at her desk, correcting papers. Gracie asked if she could take Burniss' books home to her.

Instead of answering, Mrs. Coatum said, "Grace, your behavior has been less than good this week. I don't know what's gotten into you. You're a seventh-grader. You seem to have forgotten it. I expect you older girls to set an example.

"I find no handwriting paper among these. There was no arithmetic yesterday. You and Nanny Olive Moore played during geography today, and there was that silliness in the cloakroom this afternoon. It's unbecoming, Grace."

Gracie waited in silence. She hung her head. She was afraid to look up — afraid that, somehow, the tragedy of Crawford at home would leap, full-blown and recognizable, from behind her eyes.

"You may get Burniss' books," Mrs. Coatum said.

Then, as Gracie was coming up the aisle with the primer and the cut-and-paste book, Mrs. Coatum said, "It won't make an iota of difference whether poor little Burniss has the books or not."

Gracie's eyes confronted Mrs. Coatum's. Now, she was only afraid that Mrs. Coatum would read the anger over what she had just said about Burniss. Mrs. Coatum didn't even give Burniss a chance. She just grabbed her the way the boy did the tin soldier in the fairy tale, and threw her into the fire the way the boy did the soldier. Threw the one-legged tin soldier into the fire. The one-legged . . .

Lizzie was put out with her, and they walked in silence all the way home. The minute they were in their yard, Lizzie yanked loose from Gracie. From well across the yard, she turned and yelled back, "Gracie stinks." Then she scuttled for the back door.

Gracie angled away from the house, intending to sit on the swing tied to a cherry tree down toward the road. The waning afternoon sun splashed the sky with color. The cherry tree limbs were black against the horizon. Gracie settled on the fall-damp swing board and hooked her elbows around the ropes, putting her cold hands into the pockets of her jacket. The grass under the swing had been worn away by feet pushing. She ticked a toe in the mud and made herself sway — only a little, because the cold teased her. Soon, though, she had a need to go higher and higher. She gouged her toe into the slick, hauled on the ropes with red hands, and threw her head back until her braids swung. She would go until her toe touched that branch. That one.

Someone gripped the swing board from behind, and her body surged. As she sailed out, she twisted her head to see who.

"Hang on," he grunted, poised to catch the board when she flew back within reach.

"Push me hard, Dad — hard as you can. I want to touch a branch."

He pushed her so far that her feet burst in among the branches. Then she swept down, and he grabbed her ankles and ran under her and turned, laughing, and she laughed back. At the next outward reach of the swing, she catapulted off and landed on stinging feet and tipped over onto the autumn grass. He pulled her up.

Somehow, by common consent, the two of them headed for the lake, leaving her book bag and lunch pail roosting under the cherry tree. They walked all the way to the lake in silence. When they got there, they leaned on a boat turned turtle on the sand. He sheltered her from the wind with his arm.

She stood thinking. She wanted to say to him, Dad, Crawford makes me sad, too. Like you, I wish it had never happened. I want him to have two feet. That's what I want more than anything else in the world —

for Crawford to have two feet. She looked up at him. He looked down and she had to smile that awful smile that has tears pushing behind it. Gracie ducked her head and made a little square smooth place in the cold sand with her toe.

By and by she said, "Dad, are you still planning to order chicks in the spring like you said you might and us raise them in the garage and all that?"

"Yep," he said. "You know, you've got to get that half of the garage cleaned up so we can build a pen and set up the brooder. We'll make some kind of a rig with hardware cloth to keep the babies up out of drafts at first."

"I might start redding up that part of the garage tomorrow," Gracie said. She watched a gull swoop. "Dad," she said, "you know what I want you to do this summer?"

"What?" he asked.

"Teach me the Australian crawl. I'm past the stage in life of the dog paddle. How soon you think the lake'll warm up enough to go swimming? April? Sooner?"

"April! You'd freeze your bedackit, I guarantee. How about the last week of June, first week of July?"

"Is that a promise?"

"That's a promise."

She got to shivering then because the wind was so cold. Finally, she had to laugh at the way her teeth were chattering. He captured one of her cold hands and they headed for home, running.

10

Every day Mama did the same things for Crawford. She boiled bottles and made formula. She bathed him, her hands capable and gentle as they turned his strange little body this way and that. She washed his clothes and diapers. If he was fretful with colic, she walked with him or rocked him. For the most part, she did it in silence. Just once, when Mama didn't know anybody was about, Gracie heard her cooing to Crawford:

> "Hi dopie dilly dock,
> Pennyroyal tea,
> Crawford's got the bellyache
> And, oh dear me."

Crawford had a lot of colic — mostly in the evenings around suppertime. One evening, the potatoes scorched because Mama was in the living room trying to soothe Crawford. At the supper table, both Lizzie and Roberta poked through the bowl to see if there was a good potato. Since there wasn't, they sent the bowl on around without taking any.

Mama was sitting at the end of the table with Crawford across her lap. Above his crying, she said, "Just what do you plan to fill up on, Lizzie and Roberta?"

Lizzie dutifully jabbed a potato and set it on her plate, well away from her peas and salmon patty. Silently, Gracie doctored her own potato with ketchup.

Daddy saw that Roberta wasn't going to take a potato, so he reached over and put one on her plate.

"Listen here," he said. "Mama tries hard to fix supper. It's hard with the baby. The potatoes are browned down a little bit; that's all. They're perfectly good to eat."

Out of the corner of her eye, Gracie could see how still Roberta was sitting. Hu was smashing peas on the highchair tray. Crawford was wailing and making the blue blanket he was wrapped in rise and fall with his distress.

Suddenly Roberta scraped her chair back and stood up. Over Gracie's head she said, "The baby makes me sick." Gracie knew what Roberta was saying, but Daddy pretended he didn't.

He jumped up, saying, "Well, it's the first time babies have made you sick." He grabbed the dishtowel and began to clear smashed peas from Hu's tray. He wiped her hands frantically. Gracie prayed that Roberta wouldn't say anything else.

Roberta's words crashed down on her head. "I don't mean Hu, Daddy," she said. "I mean Crawford — him and his . . . and his . . . one foot! That's what I can't stand."

Daddy reached across the table, spilling Lizzie's milk. He took Roberta by the shoulders and shook her. "Do you think anybody can stand it?" he said.

"Robert!" Mama cried.

Daddy left the kitchen, slamming the back door and leaving a huge silence that Gracie could hear over Roberta's and Crawford's crying. He hadn't taken his coat out of the cellar-way. From her place at the table, Gracie could see the Plymouth's lights stab darkness this way and that as he backed and turned and then fled down the driveway. Across from her, Lizzie sat sucking her thumb and looking at the puddle of her milk on the oilcloth. Crawford's blanket blotted up Mama's tears as they fell. Roberta was behind her hands, crying.

Gracie felt as though she were all alone in the kitchen. The words potato, salmon patty, peas, potato, salmon patty, peas, spun in her head.

The words still echoed later while she was trying to get Hu ready for bed. Hu wanted Mama and wouldn't settle for "This little piggy" or "Here sits the Lord Mayor" or any of it. Finally Mama came out of her bedroom with Crawford still on her arm. She picked up the tail of her apron to wipe her eyes, then handed Crawford to Gracie and picked up Hulene.

"Poor little Huie," Mama said and put her face down against Hu. Gracie thought it would be mean to watch sorrow that Mama just wanted to hide against Hu, so she took Crawford and went down the hall to her own room.

Gracie had never offered to hold Crawford — not once since he had come home from the hospital. She couldn't stand him, either — the same as Roberta — the same as Daddy.

She pushed her door to, skirted the card table that held her collections, and sat down on the edge of her bed with the baby. She was surprised at how heavy he was. Her nose picked up his curds-and-whey smell.

He didn't have much hair, but because it was so dark, it was easy to see the shape it would take when it grew. There was a cowlick on one side of his forehead. His eyes were clear blue and wide set. He had that same little dent in the middle of his chin that Daddy had and that she had herself.

Her eyes pieced out the rest of him. It was easy to imagine two good legs and feet under the blanket. He was sucking his fist. He didn't know there was anything the matter with him. All he knew was that he wanted to suck his fist. Gracie felt like crying for him. The next instant, she couldn't stand him again. She got a terrible pain right between her shoulders and had to shift Crawford to ease it. That made his fist fall away from his mouth and he couldn't make it go back. He butted his blanket with his foot and began to cry loudly.

"Shh-sh-sh," Gracie whispered, jiggling him. Soon, Mama came to the door. Without looking up, Gracie said, "I guess he's hungry."

"Yes," Mama said. Her voice was thin. She cleared her throat and bent to pick Crawford up. "You want your supper, don't you?" she said to him.

To Gracie, it seemed as though Crawford's hunger was the only thing in the whole world that could be spoken of. She and Mama bobbed it back and forth between them like a cork while both of them were drowning in an ocean of worry about Daddy's leaving like that. Without even his coat. In December.

"Crawford takes six ounces of formula already," Mama said.

"He's heavy."

"He's a good eater. That helps him sleep through the night. He sleeps through far earlier than Hu did. She was four or five months old before she gave up her night feeding."

"Yes."

What Gracie really wanted to say was, Mama, where did Dad go? Will he be back? What do you think about it? What shall I think about it?

"I'll feed this little boy," Mama said. "Gracie, better get to bed." Mama pulled the door shut again behind her.

Gracie spread her dress over a chair and threaded her undershirt down over the bedpost. She got into her pajamas and stood for a minute straightening the things on her collection table. Then she got into bed.

Usually when Daddy was on an evening shift at G.E., Gracie could hear Mama catching up on things around the house. She could hear the muted slap of the iron against the padded board and the clang as Mama placed it on the metal iron rest. Some nights Mama sang while she worked, but tonight the house was large with silence.

Once, Gracie woke into the silence and tiptoed into Lizzie and Hu's room to look out their window onto the drive. She stared through the black glass, trying to see if the Plymouth was parked out there. Maybe she'd slept through his coming home.

Long after she'd gotten back in bed, she was cold. It seemed as though the empty drive had frozen her through.

Later, she was jerked awake by a cry from Roberta.

Gracie struggled to her feet, not even aware of what she was doing.

"Gracie! Gracie, get Mama!" Roberta cried. Gracie stumbled into the bathroom, the light punishing her eyes. Roberta was sitting on the toilet with her pajama pants on the floor at her feet, a cross of blood at the crotch.

Gracie banged out of the bathroom and ran to Mama's room down the hall. "Mama!" she cried into darkness, "Roberta's hurt!"

"Oh my, oh my," Mama breathed as she stumbled past Gracie.

Gracie followed the sound of Crawford's whimpering to his wicker bassinet. She was shaking so that her feet wouldn't stay close to the floor while she creaked Crawford back and forth.

In a minute, Mama was back, turning on the pink bed lamp. "It's all right; it's all right," she said to herself and Gracie.

"What happened to Roberta?" Gracie's words sounded queer, strained through shivering.

"Gracie, she's fine. She's all right. She's finally come round, that's all. Turned into a woman." Mama rummaged through the top drawer of her dresser and her eyes met Gracie's in the mirror. She left off rummaging and took her old brown bathrobe off the foot of the bed. She put it around Gracie, pulled her close for a moment, and left a kiss in her hair as she turned back to the dresser.

"Now, dagnabit, what did I do with it? Oh, here."

Mama found what she was searching for and went back to Roberta in the bathroom.

A little while later, both of them came down the hall. Roberta sat on the edge of Mama and Daddy's bed. "Oh, Mama," she said, "that scared me out of my wits!" Roberta was shaking, too. Mama threw the covers over her lap. "I was wishing it would happen, and then when it did, it scared me half to death." Roberta laughed a jagged laugh.

Roberta said to Gracie, "Here I turned into a woman — just like that." She snapped her fingers.

"Well, not just like that," Mama said, snapping her fingers and patting Roberta's knee. "It's been coming on — like a wave way out on the lake and making its way ashore. It's been coming on; I've known. And it's coming on Gracie, too."

Roberta said, "Gracie, you should see the rig you have to wear." After a moment, she added, "Oh, I guess it's not too bad."

"Of course it's not," Mama said. "Here we all sit rattling like old Brom Bones. I think we'd better get to bed. It's cold."

Gracie heard the clock in the dining room strike four and, later, five. She wondered if Mama would tell Daddy what had happened to Roberta. Was that the sort of news mothers told fathers — the way they did when the baby cut a tooth or walked all the way across the kitchen for the first time? Did mothers tell when their daughters crossed from being a child to being a woman, and a cross of blood was what made the difference? She imagined Mama waiting for Daddy to come home, keeping the news like a gift for him.

She wondered who had first told Daddy about Crawford. Mama? Here the two of them had had that news eating in their hearts for ten days, the ten days between the time Crawford was born and the day he came home from the hospital.

Gracie tried to think about the storm that must have swept Mama and Daddy during those days when Mama and Crawford were in the hospital. Had Mama said the words that she had whispered to Gracie the other night: "Don't be sorry for Crawford. He's a lovely baby. He'll grow and blossom — you'll see." Maybe Daddy had shouted at Mama the words Gracie had wanted to say: "He's not lovely. He's a crippled baby." The thoughts were scalding. Gracie tried to shut them off.

II

Mama was up well before Saturday was on its feet. The ring of gas flame under the tea kettle made a warm bright spot in the kitchen. Roberta was sitting at the table with her head down on her arms.

"Some warm tea will help," Mama said.

"I don't know as I like this turning into a woman," Roberta said, her voice muffled. "My stomach hurts."

"It won't bother long," Mama said, putting a brown sugar belly button on Hu's oatmeal. The minute Mama turned to make Roberta's tea, Hu ate the lump of sugar. Then she stretched to set her oatmeal bowl off the highchair tray and onto the table. It spilled over the things Lizzie was cutting out of the old Sears Roebuck catalog.

"Mama, Hu wrecked my cutouts. Bad, Hu," Lizzie said, setting the gooey bowl back on the tray.

Gracie took the bowl before Hu pushed it onto the floor. "Come on, you skinny-minny," she coaxed. She took a tiny bite of the cereal herself and then offered one to Hulene. "Mmm, this is good," Gracie said, rubbing her stomach.

"Mmm," Hu said, taking a taste of the oatmeal. She rubbed her stomach, but then her face clouded. "No, bad," she said, pushing the bowl away.

"Make her some toast, Gracie," Mama said.

Later, Roberta stayed upstairs to keep an eye on things, and Mama and Gracie went down-cellar to do the wash. Gracie tried to help Mama sort the clothes into piles. It was hard to decide, though, which things were light-colored and which were dark-colored. Mama didn't have to decide; she knew.

Mama took the gaudy Oxydol box off the shelf and measured soap into the churning washing machine. Steam and clean soap smell filled the cellar. Gracie followed Mama's ring-around-the-rosy of clothes out of the suds and into the first rinse, out of the first rinse and into the second. Mama poked the clothes through the wringer, and Gracie caught them and dropped them into the bushel basket on the floor.

Suddenly, Gracie asked, "Will Daddy come home

today?" She wanted Mama to say "Yes" right off the bat, the way she dropped Roberta's brown and yellow plaid dress into the light-colored pile without seeming to wonder if the brown in it qualified it for dark-colored.

Mama reversed the wringer before it stripped the buttons off Lizzie's dress. She held the dress up, shook it, and folded it so that the buttons were padded. She poked the dress into the wringer by its collar. "I expect he will," she said.

But I want to *know* he will, Gracie thought.

The washer went on jerking the clothes back and forth. Grun-grun, grun-grun, grun-grun. Gracie kept her eyes on the flattened clothes that roped out of the wringer. Mama fed the wringer's jaws.

The words Gracie had wanted to hear were all there in her own head. She had wanted Mama to say, Why, of course he'll be back. When that pot of chicken noodle soup goes on the table for lunch, he'll be right in his place at the table.

"I'd better hang, Ma; the basket's getting full," Gracie said. She picked up the heavy basket and lugged it over to where the clotheslines were strung.

When Gracie and Mama went upstairs at noon, Roberta had set the table and made the soup. She was standing by the table with the pot in one hand and the ladle in the other. "You want two scoops or one, Gracie?" she asked.

When she had dished up Mama's and Gracie's soup, she stood uncertainly, the ladle still in her hand. She looked sorrowfully at Daddy's place at the head of the table. "Should I dish up for Daddy, Mama?" she asked.

"I guess not," Mama said, and her soft words confirmed the emptiness.

He didn't come. After lunch, Gracie and Roberta played Authors. Politely, they said *The Prince and the Pauper*, not *The Prince and the Pooper*, as they always did. Roberta didn't say a word about Gracie's having bent the corner of *Little Women* on purpose to spite Roberta the first day they had had the cards. Gracie wondered if Roberta was always going to be polite now because she had grown up in the night. She hoped not.

After two games, Roberta said, no, she didn't want to play another; her belly ached. Would Gracie mind going upstairs and getting *Little Women* off her dresser? She wanted to lie on the couch and read "The Valley of the Shadow"—the chapter where Beth died.

Gracie didn't feel up to saying, Who was your servant last year; go get it yourself. Instead, she went upstairs and brought down the book and also Roberta's bathrobe so that she could cover up. When she flapped the bathrobe over her, Roberta squawked, "Quit fanning me! I'm cold enough already."

Gracie gave her another flap, and Roberta yelled, "Mama! Gracie's acting up!"

Gracie faded from the living room. She got her jacket out of the cellar-way, careful not to let her eyes see Daddy's jacket still hanging there. She went out and shut herself in the garage. It was cold enough that she pulled her wadded mittens out of her pockets and put them on.

First, she put all the tools neatly between the studs in the garage wall. Then she arranged the grape-picking carts against the back wall and stacked the old *Liberty* and *Saturday Evening Post* magazines on them. She begrudged the tricycles the room they took up with their handlebars and pedals akimbo, dumb awkward things. Daddy said after the war she and Roberta would get bicycles. It was too hard to get one now. You had to have some reason besides wanting to ride to the lake or to school if your mother would let you. You had to have a reason, like needing a bicycle to get to and from your job, and even then there was a lot of red tape involved. Gracie sighed. Probably when the war was over, she and Roberta would be too old to care whether they had two-wheelers or not. That was one aspect of growing up that was bad.

A huge leggy spider crawled out of the boot that Gracie had picked up. "Eeek!" she squealed and threw the boot down. She took a rake and used the handle to poke the boot back under the grape-picking carts.

The spider started her talking to herself. "I bet it was a black widow. Dad says he's going to order a hundred and fifty baby chickens. That's a lot. Mama says Leghorns are the best layers. I still like the looks of the Barred Rocks. Daddy says he hasn't made up his mind about what kind to get yet. Anyway, if we sell some of them for broilers, it doesn't matter if they're good layers or not. In fact, heavier chickens would be better. The pictures of the Leghorns in *The Farm Journal* — they always look so skinny." Gracie examined the garage ceiling, speculating on where they could locate the brooder to take the best advantage of the light socket. "Right here in the center it has to be, I guess."

She got the stiff old garage broom and began sweeping the dust into a pile on the floor, scrubbing at an oil stain. Suddenly, behind her, the garage door rattled up on its metal track. It was Daddy. She was so surprised that she wasn't sure what to say. She spread out an arm and introduced him to the clean half of the garage. "How do you like it?" she said. "You think this is good enough? Is there going to be room for a hundred and fifty? I think the brooder has to go right here in the middle, don't you? That's the only place we can plug it in. Oh! We could use an extension cord; I didn't think about that."

"No, I think the middle's fine," he said. "That way, we can move all around the brooder. I plan to build a platform up off the floor about this high." He measured a place on the wall with his hand to show her. "Little chicks aren't as puny about drafts as little turkeys are, but just the same, we want to take the best care of the little critters that we can."

"Have you thought any more about what kind we should order?" she asked him. "What's the other name for Barred Rocks?"

"Plymouth Rocks," he said.

"Plymouth," she said. "I couldn't think of that for the life of me."

They puttered around the garage, arranging things. "Watch out for that boot," Gracie told him; "there's a black widow in it."

"No," he said, smiling at her.

"Yeah, one jumped out at me. It was as big as an octopus."

"Black widows are small," he said. "It was probably a wolf spider."

"Well, it was a killer, whatever it was. It gave me the willies." She shuddered and drew her lips back away from her teeth so that the cords on her neck tightened.

He sniffed laughter out through his nose. Then suddenly, his face looked troubled. The talk of chickens and spiders dwindled to nothing. The magic went out of the garage. He dusted off his hands a little bit and held the side door open for her.

Gracie followed him into the house, thinking how hard it was to go back to people after trouble. There was a tiptoe, don't-touch-me meanness about it. It was hard. You wanted to pick up where you'd left off before the trouble, but you couldn't look people in the eye.

She felt sorry for Daddy. When you'd gone and told how you really felt, the way Daddy had done, and Roberta, too, then you had to go on holding that heavy thing out in front of you. It hurt more, she was sure, to have it unsaid, in your heart, but it wasn't so dangerous. She wished there were some way to erase Friday's supper and all that had happened. She wished they could all turn back from the path that Roberta had pushed them onto. While she was at it, she might as well wish them on back before the time when Crawford was born. Wish he never was.

Daddy washed his hands at the sink and then settled

heavily in his chair at the head of the table. Hu soon discovered that he was home. When she ran to him, he tilted his chair back on its hind legs and lifted her into his lap. Gracie got herself a drink of water, not wanting it. When Mama came into the kitchen to start supper, Gracie left.

Mama and Daddy's talk was stiff and dry. Gracie wanted to be out of reach of it. Roberta was upstairs with her door shut. At last, Gracie sought the sanctuary of noise in front of the radio with Lizzie.

Not long after, Mama called to Gracie to come and set the table. From the hall, Gracie heard Mama say, "Never once, never once, Robert Prayther, have you held him or fed a bottle or changed a diaper, and I'm ashamed of you."

As she set cups in a row on the oilcloth, Gracie could see Daddy's face out of the corner of her eye. It was a pale mask, his eyes hot and angry behind it. Hu was dizzying around on his lap, trying to slide to the floor head-first. Daddy eased her down, saying, "Whoopsy-daisy, Huie."

Hulene righted herself, climbed aboard Daddy's shoe, and held up her arms to be lifted. "Uppy, uppy," she said. When Daddy took her up, she stood and looked into his face for a minute and then put her head down on his shoulder. Around them, and around Mama's fierce silence, Gracie set the plates on the table.

Roberta came down to supper, but she didn't look at anybody. She didn't complain and fish the tomatoes out of her macaroni as usual. She ate them. Daddy filled his plate twice and ate hungrily. Mama sat rearranging the food on her plate, not eating it to speak of. Suddenly she pushed her chair back and left the table. Daddy looked up in surprise. Then he got up and followed Mama, saying, "Watch Hu, girls; don't let her fall."

As soon as Daddy was out of sight, Hu stood up in the highchair. Gracie took her onto her lap, letting her play with the uneaten macaroni on her plate.

After a little bit, Gracie and Roberta got up and scraped all the uneaten food into the garbage can and did the dishes in silence. Gracie could feel fear settling inside her.

They turned off the kitchen light and went into the living room. Roberta turned on the lamp and Lizzie fiddled with the radio's dials. A program bounded into the living room, the noise making even Hu put her hands over her ears.

Roberta scolded, "For Pete's sake, Lizzie, you've got it turned up to glory." She jumped for the radio and twisted the noise to nothing. "I'll dial the program; you leave the radio alone."

"Okay, okay," said Lizzie. She sat on the floor and put her thumb in her mouth.

Later, when Hu was tired and whining, Gracie took her upstairs. Because Hu's Dr. Denton's were in Mama and Daddy's room, Gracie put her to bed in her clothes, taking her shoes off but leaving her socks on to keep her feet warm. Then she tiptoed down the hall to her own room and closed the door quietly, shutting out the last stain of light that came up from the living room.

As she stood with her back to her room, the doorknob still cold in her hand, Gracie's thoughts came rushing in. What if Daddy decides to go away for good because of Crawford? What will Mama do? What will become of us?

She turned and started across her room in the dark. Angling a little to miss her collection table, she collided sharply with something in the aisle between her bed and the table. Her skin stung all over with the shock of it. She put out her hands, and her fingers felt the mesh of Crawford's bassinet. What is this doing in my room? she wondered, backing and searching for the light switch.

The bassinet loomed large and awkward in the narrow aisle. Crawford had wakened when she bumped into his bed. He was lying on his stomach, but he was bobbing his head up a little and moving it around, snuffling. Either Mama or Daddy must have put him in here — must have pushed him out of their room. As Gracie stood looking down at the baby, she remembered Uncle Hugh's saying, "Get it out of here — go dump it under a bush."

She picked Crawford up and sank onto the edge of her bed, leaning over a little to muffle his noise if he couldn't be quieted. He turned toward her warmth, though, and sagged again into sleep. She sat holding him and listening. Once, she heard the searing sound of grown-up crying. Later, she heard Lizzie talking to herself in the bathroom before she went into the room she shared with Hu to go to bed. Below, Roberta finally turned off the radio and came up and shut herself into her bedroom at the head of the stairs. Cold crept up Gracie's back. Each of her toes, inside her shoes, seemed to be separate with cold.

At last, she got up to ease Crawford back into the bassinet. She measured each movement, giving him time to accept, and begging him to stay asleep. He struck out immediately against the cold circle of his basket, and she had to pick him up again. Holding him with one arm, she turned off the light and felt her way back to the bed. She poked her shoes off by the heels, first one foot and then the other, and then, inch by inch, crept into bed with him still packaged on her arm. He grumbled about the cold sheet.

"Come on, don't get all excited," she whispered. "You have to be good. Look, I'm still here. I didn't put you back in your old basket. Listen, you'd better not wet on my bed — that's the only thing." She felt almost sorry when he stilled with sleep.

She lay beside him, her thoughts whipping her back and forth. Suppose it was Mama who'd put him in her room? So far, it was only Mama who seemed to stick up for Crawford. What if Mama couldn't stand him either? What if taking care of him was just a case of buckling down and doing what had to be done? Mama could do that. She had canned grape juice even when her belly was so big that she had to stand way back from the stove. "Why, you'll not catch me letting all these grapes go to waste," she'd said.

Gracie's thoughts shifted to Crawford. She didn't see why God went and left him unfinished the way He did. It would have been so easy to make Crawford perfect. Then everybody would have been happy.

The Praythers were not churchgoers. Not like Nanny Olive and her family. The Moores went to church every Sunday and sometimes other days, too. Their church followed them around, not letting them eat meat on Fridays. Once, Nanny Olive, forgetting it was the end of the week, had eaten half of Gracie's baloney sandwich. Afterward, she'd said, "With this baloney sandwich in my stomach on Friday, I'm a walking sin, just like you, Earl."

"Want me to squeeze it out of you?" Earl had offered.

"No thanks," Nanny Olive answered.

Once in a while, Roberta and Gracie would go to Sunday school, but never often enough to find out the conclusions to the continued stories in the Sunday school papers they were given. Gracie had never known Mama and Daddy to go to church. Maybe if all the Praythers had gone to church, this wouldn't have happened to Crawford. Maybe it was a punishment.

Gracie lay beside Crawford, wishing — careful not to let the word "miracle" into her mind at first. She found she couldn't help thinking about miracles, though.

When she was seven, she had gotten a new box of crayons and a Deanna Durbin coloring book. Before she started to color, she promised herself that she wouldn't go out of the lines and she wouldn't break any of the crayons. The red crayon broke while she was coloring Deanna Durbin's skirt on the very first page. She could have cried. Instead, she got a pencil and poked the two sections of crayon out of their little tubes of paper. She laid the crayon pieces on the dining room windowsill, squeezed her eyes shut, and prayed for the miracle of a whole crayon. Then she'd gone into the kitchen to give the miracle time to work. She diddled around out there until Mama said, "Gracie, what are you up to?"

"Nothing," Gracie said. She'd gone back into the dining room and, with her eyes shut, moved to the windowsill. When her eyes snapped open, the red crayon was still in two pieces. She remembered that she was not particularly surprised. She also remembered that it didn't make her stop believing that there was such a thing as a miracle. It didn't make sense. She guessed now that even at seven, she could tell that a red crayon wasn't worth a miracle. Crawford was. And Wreath said... If she only had someone to believe with her that the Batten Woman could work miracles... Well, Nanny Olive's grandmother...

Gracie drifted to sleep. In a dream, she *saw* Crawford's toes — all ten of them. Ten little pink buds on his feet. Wreath Robinson was saying, "Did you hear about Stella Edwards and the Praythers' baby?" Even in her sleep, Gracie could feel her skin prickling with goose flesh.

"Oh-h," she heard herself saying aloud, as she woke up.

12

Wonder and excitement were mushrooming inside Gracie. Beside her, Crawford was squirming awake, squeaking, working himself up to a cry. The picture of ten pink toes sprang into her mind. It's as real as real, she thought. I can just *see* his other foot. If part of what makes a miracle work is wanting it bad enough . . .

"Hey, you, what's the matter? You hungry?" she whispered to him. He didn't listen — just went on jabbing around under the blankets and getting louder and louder. She jumped out of bed and scooped him into her arms and tiptoed downstairs. She shut both the pantry and kitchen doors to keep the sounds of his crying from going upstairs while she fixed his bottle.

As she diapered him, she tried to stifle the fright that she always felt when she saw his short leg. She let her eyes linger on it, believing with all her strength that her dream could come true and that he could have two feet. I think my dream was a sign, she said to herself — a sign to take him to the Batten Woman. If the Batten Woman could bring a baby back from the dead . . . Gracie touched the firm little toes of Crawford's foot. He drew his knee up sharply and kicked and howled. Behind Gracie, his bottle sizzled to a boil. She had to put Crawford off while she cooled the milk at the sink, being careful that the sharp cold of the water didn't break the glass bottle.

Crawford gobbled his breakfast hungrily. She wiped some milk off his chin and nighty and hurried to get his bonnet and sweater and quilt out of the end of the buffet. She bundled Crawford and then drove her arms into her own coat and buttoned it with clumsy shaking fingers. It was beginning to snow a little bit.

It wasn't until she had turned onto Miller Road with Crawford that some doubts began. He was heavy. Mama might be mad at her for taking him out in the snow. Gracie couldn't bring into focus a picture of herself knocking on the Batten Woman's door with Crawford in her arms. What in the world was she going to say, anyway?

Then she thought of Daddy leaving the house Friday with no coat and not coming back until yesterday afternoon. She thought of him and Mama fighting about Crawford and of Crawford getting pushed out into her room. The need for a miracle bit into her. She was going to the Batten Woman's. No matter what, she was going.

A northeast wind was badgering the Batten Woman's chicken and guinea coops. Gracie's breath made little clouds as she climbed over the fence. She rounded the corner of the building and knocked at the door. She would have run away if the door hadn't been answered almost immediately.

"What do you want?" There was no friendliness in the Batten Woman's voice or her eyes. Her hair was in one braid, thin and gray as a rat's tail. The skin of her face was ill-fitting, loose and wrinkled. She was dressed in an old wrapper and slippers.

"I . . . this . . ." Gracie squeaked. Her face apologized for Crawford.

The Batten Woman looked irritated by the cold air swirling in around her feet. She drew Gracie inside the barnlike room and closed the door behind her. A kerosene stove gave the room a bad smell. There was clutter everywhere.

Oh, how could I have done this? How could I have come here? Gracie thought.

Gracie didn't give Crawford to the Batten Woman; the old woman took him. After pushing aside dirty dishes to make room, she laid him on a heavy round table. Her hands dipped and plucked like a crow working on a dead squirrel on the road as she unwrapped him.

Gracie moved closer, spurting out words. "I heard you were a healer. I heard you could heal people. Nanny Olive Moore is my best friend. Her brother . . . She said . . . Wreath Robinson told me about a baby that was dead and you brought it back to life." She might as well not have been there, for all the attention the Batten Woman seemed to be paying to her.

The Batten Woman unwrapped Crawford in his milk-stained nighty and one blue crocheted bootie, and silence clapped in the room like thunder. She turned and took Gracie by the arm. "Why did you come here?"

"I don't know," Gracie whispered.

"You don't know why you came here? I'll tell you

why you came to me. You came to Stella Edwards for a miracle. Isn't that why you came?"

Gracie shook her head. Kept shaking it and shaking it.

"For a miracle!" The Batten Woman's voice leaped. Then she pounced at Gracie again. "Who is this baby?"

"My brother, Crawford," Gracie whispered.

"Your brother." The Batten Woman shook Gracie again. "And you think you'll do this boy a favor, don't you? You'll get him a miracle to crutch his way through his life with! Well, let me tell you — there's no such thing as a miracle." The Batten Woman's eyes caught Gracie's. "And if there were such a thing as a miracle, it would be a sin to lay the heavy weight of it on that innocent baby." Gracie backed, even though the Batten Woman still had her by the arm.

"A miracle would lie on that baby like a cross, do you hear me?"

"Yes," Gracie whispered.

"Do you know the weight of a cross?"

Gracie shook her head.

"Who is this baby?"

"My brother," Gracie whispered again. The whisper raked her dry throat.

"*Who* is this baby?" the Batten Woman ranted. She let go of Gracie and cried up into the rafters, "Who *is* this baby?"

Gracie lunged at the table. She scratched the quilt around Crawford and, grabbing him up, jumped to the door. She almost fell out into the yard. The wind made Crawford gasp, and he struggled in her arms as she ran around the house and across the clean snow.

As she straddled the fence, fear and haste pumped a steady stream of little "ohs" from her.

When Gracie got home, Roberta was the only one who was up. She was hunkered over the dining room register, reading the Sunday funnies. Dionne was sitting beside her, waiting for Roberta to move so that she could have the register and its warmth.

"Wait'll you read 'Dick Tracy,' " Roberta said, her hair falling forward as she leaned on the paper with her elbows. Finally she looked up and said, in surprise, "Hey! What are you doing? You took the baby out in the snow?" Roberta's face said clearly that she thought Gracie was crazy.

"What do you care?" Gracie said.

"Is he okay?" Roberta asked.

"Yes," Gracie said.

"You want some of the funnies?"

"No."

By the time Gracie got Crawford packaged in a dry blanket, she felt weak and watery. She went into the living room and sat in the rocking chair, rocking him. The rockers began to squeak the Batten Woman's words again: "Who is this baby who is this baby who is this baby?"

Gracie felt like yelling to high heaven, "He's my brother, Crawford Charles Prayther!" She wanted to drown out the Batten Woman's crazy words.

Breakfast was strained and awkward. Hu filled the kitchen with her prattle, pleased to do all the talking, sometimes nagging words out of Mama or Daddy. After breakfast, Daddy went into the living room, far from Mama, to read the paper. Usually, he sat at the table Sunday mornings, reading the paper to Mama while she worked on the dinner. They would laugh at this or that or murmur solemnly about the war news.

Lizzie wanted to go out in the snow. Roberta was already dressed to go out, so Gracie started to put her things on, too. Everyone would have thought it was funny if she hadn't. Her mittens were still wet from the trip to the Batten Woman's, and they felt cold and ugly against her skin. By the time Gracie was ready, all Lizzie had done was to pile her things on the hall floor. She sat on the second step and insisted, "Roberta, help me."

"Oh, Lizzie," Roberta groaned, "you're such a baby. Get your own stuff on."

Sighing, Lizzie picked up her snowpants. She pushed her foot into the blue wool pants and her shoe stuck. "Look," she whined.

"You're supposed to point your toe, you dummy," Roberta said, grabbing Lizzie's pants leg and trying to pull the snowpants back off. Lizzie skidded off the steps, bellowing for Mama.

Daddy came out of the living room. "What's the trouble here?" he said.

"Oh, she's impossible," Roberta said, pointing to Lizzie.

As Gracie watched Daddy kneel and work Lizzie's foot loose, the good safe clamor of the family began to melt the fright that still lay within her. Hulene tackled Daddy's back. "Hat, coat, go out," she said.

"Okay, you go get your things, Huie," he told her.

While Daddy helped Lizzie, Roberta and Gracie put Hu into her snowsuit. "I'll meet you," Daddy said, poking them all out through the front door.

Soon, he came around the house. He had a cardboard box and a piece of Mama's clothesline. He made a box sled for Hu, and they hauled her back past the vineyard and all the way to the hill behind the garden spot. Gracie walked with her back to the wind. She noticed their tracks on the snow — like a clutch of little gray birds following a dribble of corn. Only Mama and Crawford were off alone in the house.

When they came back to the yard, Lizzie made a snow angel. "Haul me up out of this angel so I won't mess it up," she said up into Daddy's face. He reached out his long arms and lifted her.

"Hey, Dad, let's have us a snowball fight," Roberta said, dancing backward with her mittened hands full of soft snow. Laughing, she flung the snow in the air, showering it down on Daddy. He shoveled up snow with his hands and arms and ran after Roberta. "Ha, ha, can't catch me," she shouted, but he caught her just the same. She rolled in the snow like a puppy.

Gracie stood with the wind nagging her. She wiped her nose with her mitten. Once, when Hu was practically as young as Crawford, Daddy had bundled her all up and brought her out for a ride in a box in the snow. Gracie pictured Crawford inside in his buggy. It was too bad he had to miss the white snow and the rainbow of laughing and silliness arched over it.

Suddenly Daddy came running up and hugged Gracie. "You're cold; you're frozen stiff," he said. "Come on, let's go in."

It occurred to Gracie as they went inside that she had never before gone in from playing in snow without having to be broomed off first.

13

Monday and Tuesday in mid-December were teachers' institute days. Mrs. Coatum would be attending meetings, so school would be closed.

Daddy had decided to take advantage of the school holiday. He and Mama were going in to Erie to Household Finance. While Mama was pinning her hat in place in front of the kitchen mirror, she was still arguing. "Robert, I just hate to take out another loan."

"Well, I intend to have Christmas," Daddy said.

"We don't know what expenses we face with the baby," Mama insisted.

"The girls are going to have Christmas or my name's not Robert Prayther."

"Well, maybe your name's *not* Robert Prayther; you seem a stranger to me," Mama said.

Daddy looked at her sharply. His face was stern and strange. "You girls see that you take care of things here," he said to Roberta and Gracie. He started to take

Mama's arm as they went to the door, but she pulled away from him.

When they were gone, Gracie took refuge in the little bathroom under the steps. Why were Mama and Daddy so mean to each other? Why was Mama against Christmas? Why hadn't Daddy said, "The girls and Crawford are going to have Christmas . . ."? I wish it was back in the time when I knew Christmas came from Santa Claus and not from Household Finance, Gracie thought. She squeezed her eyelids shut and imagined Santa Claus piling up a lavish heap of toys for Crawford — everything he could think of, and then some. All the Praythers would be surprised on Christmas morning, *all* of them, and rejoicing would be easy.

Gracie heard the phone ringing in the hall. Hu and Lizzie were yelling at one another, and Roberta was shouting at them to keep quiet. Gracie's eyes snapped open. She grabbed the *Liberty* magazine off the back of the toilet and threw it on the floor. For good measure, she kicked it under the sink, and its cover came loose.

"Gracie, will you get these kids quiet!" Roberta yelled. Gracie picked up the magazine and put it back, loose cover and all, on the back of the toilet.

Roberta, tethered by the phone cord, was holding the receiver against her stomach and threatening Lizzie and Hu, who were just beyond reach. Hu had Lizzie's primer.

"You'll tear it!" Lizzie screamed.

"For crimast sakes, will you get these two quiet so I can hear myself think," Roberta huffed. "This house is like a boiler factory! It's like a nut house!"

Gracie took the primer from Hu, holding it above her head. Hu screamed. Roberta glared at Gracie. Gracie waited for what she considered a decent interval — long enough so that Roberta could tell she'd follow orders when she got good and ready, and then she handed the primer to Lizzie and picked up Hu and took her into the living room. She sat on the couch and tapped the soles of Hu's shoes. "Pitty, patty, polt, shoe the wild colt," she whispered, listening past her own voice to what Roberta was saying in the hall.

"My parents have gone in to Erie . . . Just me and Gracie and the kids. Yeah. Well, how long do you think it would take? . . . Oh, I have enough saved up to get you-know-what . . . If you think it's boring there, you should be here! I'll be ready in two shakes of a lamb's tail. Okay, see you soon. Bye."

Wreath. Gracie knew it was Wreath.

Roberta stuck her head into the living room. "Me and Wreath are just going uptown for a little bit. I want to get something at Woolworth's. Now, don't get your dander up. When I get back, I'll change all the poops and the pees and settle all the bawlbabies' hashes and you can go shut yourself in your room or whatever you want. I'll make it up to you — I promise." She withdrew her head and tore upstairs.

"Mama'd kill you!" Gracie yelled in impotence.

Roberta's leaving just made things worse. Lizzie sat in her boom-boom in the playroom reading her primer and talking to Dick and Jane as though they were present. Gracie envied Lizzie. She lay on the couch, letting Hu climb up and down over her. She was cold, but it was too much trouble to get up and get the army blanket over on Daddy's chair. Finally, Hu settled on her chest and poked at Gracie's eyes with her finger, saying "Yie? Yie?"

Gently, Gracie touched Hu's eyelid. "Hu's yie," she said. Then she touched Hu's other eyelid. "Nose," she said. Hu looked perplexed. She sat still for a minute and then wagged her head solemnly. She put a finger on Gracie's eye and said, "Nose."

"I can't fool you, Huie, can I?" Gracie said, laughing and squeezing Hu. Overhead, Crawford woke up and began to cry.

Gracie slid Hu to the floor, and the baby followed her to the kitchen like a shadow. Gracie put the bottle on to heat. She scooped up Hu and started upstairs, trying to judge whether she had time to change Crawford before the bottle got too hot. If Hulene didn't get into trouble while she was doing it, maybe there'd be time.

The morning was impossible. Hu was bad; Crawford was worse. Lizzie started lunch on the sly and poked holes in two cans of soup. She couldn't turn the can opener on either one after she'd pressed the clamp down and punctured both lids.

"I don't even want to make soup, Lizzie," Gracie said. "How many hands do you think I have? How many things do you think I can do at once? And now we have two cans of soup opened! And they're not even the same kind!"

"One's vegetable and one's not," Lizzie murmured,

resting on her elbows on the table and reading the soup can labels with concentration.

Gracie stood with Crawford crying and squirming in her arms and Hu clinging to her leg. "Lizzie, I could just boot you one," she cried in frustration. "Get into the living room," she said, nudging her. Chagrined at her failure with the soup cans, Lizzie obeyed.

"Now, sit on that rocker and hold this baby and I don't mean maybe," Gracie said. "You hold him around his middle and don't let him fall while I take Hu up and put her to bed for her nap. You hear me?"

Lizzie sat and accepted Crawford, lacing her hands across his stomach with his head tucked under her chin. Her head was tilted back stiffly. "Shall I call you if I'm going to drop him?" she asked.

"You drop him . . ." Gracie howled, "and . . . and . . ." She snatched up Hu and ran upstairs with her. When she got back to the living room, Lizzie was sitting like a statue with the baby writhing on her lap.

"Whew," she breathed when Gracie took him.

Gracie was standing there trying to juggle Crawford and rewind his blanket when Roberta burst into the room, dancing in desperation and breathless. "Hide Crawford! Hide him quick! Don't answer me back, Gracie Prayther! Will you just listen to me and get him out of here?" She grabbed Gracie by the shoulders and pushed her toward the stairs. "Gra-cie," she pleaded in a shrill whisper. Then she turned and bounced toward the dining room.

"Coming, guys, coming — just hold your horses!" she called in an entirely different voice.

On the stairs, Gracie jiggled Crawford rhythmically to quiet him. She helped his thumb to his eager mouth. From the kitchen she heard Wreath say, "Some hostess. Slammed the door in our faces and disappeared like a shot."

"Well, I hadda see a man about a dog, for crimast sakes," Roberta said, giggling.

"Woo-woo!" Gracie heard Frank's voice. Hugging Crawford to her, she ran up the steps as though the devil were at her heels. She stood just inside her room with Crawford and listened until her ears ached.

"No, Frankie, you can't see what's in my bag," Roberta said. "It's for me to know and you to find out. Yow! What am I saying!"

"Yeah," Wreath squealed, "what *are* you saying, Brr, you dodo!"

"Come on, let me just take a peek," Frank insisted.

"Frank-ee-ee!"

For a moment Gracie was at a loss, but then it occurred to her that the bag they were talking about must be the one that contained Roberta's purchases from Woolworth's. She heard sounds like horses galloping around the dining room table and heard Lizzie yell, "Run, Roberta!"

A piece of furniture tipped over with a bump. A chorus of squeals. Gracie stood with Crawford in her arms. He was sagging in sleep, beyond the need of the thumb drifting from his mouth. He was so soundless and there was so much hubbub downstairs. They were shrieking through the hall now. There was a bloodcurdling scream, and Roberta yelped, "Lay off, Frankie!"

Gracie eased Crawford into the bassinet. She tiptoed out into the hall, closing the door behind her. As she walked down the hall, she heard all the smart aleckness go out of Roberta's voice and heard her say, "Hey, you're not allowed upstairs." Gracie moved to the head of the stairs and looked down to see Frank astride the bannister, swinging his leg over the railing onto the steps. He looked up then and saw Gracie. He hesitated and slid off the end of the bannister, and Gracie walked down the stairs. There was an uncomfortable silence until Wreath jabbed the Woolworth bag in his direction and egged, "Frank-ie."

The chase was on again. Wreath and Roberta and Frank raced back and forth past Lizzie and Gracie, squealing like Uncle Hugh's pigs at feeding time. Frank made a lunge for the bag, which was still in Wreath's hands. He caught a corner of it, and Roberta and Wreath screamed as the bag ripped open from top to bottom and a Toni Permanent and a box of Kotex tumbled onto the hall floor.

"Well, well, what have we here?" Frank said.

Roberta cried, "Wr-eath," and burst into tears, covering her face with her hands.

Wreath, her face red, said, "Frank Hunter, honestly. You have no sense of decency or privacy or anything else. Why don't you just go home, for crimast sakes?"

"How was I supposed to know?" Frank said. His face had a red strangled look. He turned abruptly and slunk out through the dining room. Gracie heard the back door close behind him.

"My whole life is ruined," Roberta wailed. She leaned

her forehead against the front door and bawled. Lizzie picked up the Toni and the Kotex box and set them on the dining room table. She rested on her elbows, trying to read the labels the way she had the soup cans'. Gracie busied herself straightening up the throw rug in the hall and picking up the fallen dining room chair.

"I gotta go," Wreath said to Roberta's back. She walked out through the dining room, being very careful not to look at Gracie.

Roberta kept leaning against the front door and crying.

The words "Well, it's your own fault" rose in Gracie's throat, but she couldn't say them, with Roberta's boxes sitting on the table, exposed and vulnerable. She took them from in front of Lizzie, and Lizzie sidled away without a word. Gracie put them on the buffet. She did a little more useless straightening and then said to Roberta, "You'd better go and wash your face before Mama and Daddy get home."

Roberta turned from the door and started upstairs. Halfway up she stopped and turned. "Where'd you put my things?" she asked. Gracie pointed to the boxes in the dining room. Roberta came down and got them. Hugging them to her chest and crying, she went upstairs to her room and closed the door.

It was too bad — what had happened to Roberta — getting embarrassed in front of her friends that way. At least they hadn't found out about Crawford.

14

Mama was a day behind in the washing because of the trip to Household Finance yesterday. Gracie went down-cellar to help her while Roberta and Lizzie watched Hu and listened out for Crawford.

The washing machine's ambitious noise filled the cellar, making Mama's silence less noticeable. It seemed to Gracie that Mama's silence wasn't as on-purpose as it had been last night. Last night when Mama and Daddy came home, Mama hadn't even asked how things had gone during the day. She'd just tied herself into her apron and set to work on supper. Roberta had come downstairs, dry-eyed, and Gracie could see her watching for an opportunity to ask if Mama would give her the home permanent over Christmas vacation maybe. Gracie knew it would take Mama to make the permanent come to pass.

Roberta hadn't mentioned the Toni during supper. At bedtime, Mama doled out a dry little kiss apiece and went to bed herself. This morning though, her silence seemed born of sadness, not anger at Daddy and Household Finance.

Gracie hung diapers. By the time she was finished, Mama had wiped up the washer and the tubs, and they went upstairs together. Roberta met them at the door. "Mama," she said, "now that I've watched the kids, would you do me a favor?" With a pleading look on her face, she showed Mama the Toni.

There was nowhere in the house to get away from the smell of Roberta's permanent. Holding her nose, Gracie said, "Mama, I'm going outside. I might go over to Nanny Olive's for a little bit."

As Gracie walked along Miller Road, she noticed that everything about it was affected by that awful trip she had taken to the Batten Woman's on Sunday. The road was spoiled. She would never feel the same about it again, she thought. And all because of that crazy old woman. Well, she was crazy herself to have counted on a miracle. Crawford was the way he was and that was that.

Gracie's feet slowed as she approached the Moores'. She recognized a dread about being with Nanny Olive. What if the present was done? What if Nanny Olive wanted to come back with Gracie to see Crawford and give him the present? She stood still, hunched against the cold afternoon, muddling about the difficulties that might come up if she went to her friend's house. Finally she kicked a stone to the road's edge and turned back.

Gracie didn't want to go home. That was the only reason she turned in at Burniss' drive. As she rapped at the Watermeisters' back door, she thought, I don't want to play with Burniss.

She must have had a troubled look on her face when Mrs. Watermeister opened the door, because Burniss' mother said, "Gracie, what is it?"

"Oh, I just thought I'd come over and play with Burniss for a little," Gracie said, angry with herself. The whole business sounded hatched-up.

"Come in." As Gracie stepped into the kitchen, Mrs. Watermeister called, "Burniss, Burniss, come see who's here."

Gracie could hear a radio playing in another room: "Phil-a-del-phia scrapple fine . . ."

Burniss appeared in the kitchen doorway and looked at Gracie as though she didn't know who she was.

"She's used to seeing you at school," Mrs. Watermeister said. Burniss slipped into the kitchen and leaned against her mother.

"Do you know who this is?" Mrs. Watermeister asked.

"Yes," Burniss said.

"Who is it?"

"Gracie."

Gracie smiled at Burniss.

"She's been in the living room listening to the radio," Mrs. Watermeister said. "I was just getting ready to stir up a cake." An open cookbook was lying on the green enamel-topped table. A cup of milk and a cup of sugar stood nearby. The kitchen was as neat as the white organdy curtain at the window.

"Maybe Gracie would like to listen to the program with you while I get the cake ready for the oven. Then maybe she'll stay and have a piece with us," Mrs. Watermeister said.

Gracie had nothing to say as she followed Burniss to the living room. There, Burniss settled in a rocking chair in front of the radio. The varnish was worn off at the bottom of the radio's cabinet where Burniss pushed against it with her toe as she rocked. Gracie perched uneasily on a straight chair against the wall.

While Burniss rocked and listened to the radio, Gracie sat looking around the room. There was a glassed-in cabinet with framed photographs neatly arranged on the shelves. Most of the pictures were of Burniss. There was one of Mr. Watermeister in his Air Force uniform. He was quite handsome, Gracie thought. In one of the pictures, Mr. and Mrs. Watermeister were hugging Burniss in between them and laughing. Burniss had one arm around each parent's neck. It was nice to know that there were some people who cared that much about Burniss. Gracie glanced over at Burniss and thought about how Wreath and Earl and Mrs. Coatum — and even Lizzie — felt about her.

Suddenly Burniss began to sing along with the radio. "Ta-ra-ra boom-de-ay." She was rocking so fast that Gracie thought the rocker was on the verge of tipping over backward. She jumped up the way she would have if it had been Hu rocking that way. There was no need though; Burniss seemed to know what she was doing. "Ta-ra-ra boom-de-ay." Her singing voice was altogether different from her speaking voice. It was high and sweet and flowed easily, as though knots had come untied. Gracie sank down onto the chair again. When the song was finished, she said, "Wow, Burn, you're a good singer."

The rocking petered to a standstill. There was no more music on the radio. Burniss got up and snapped it off. It made the room so silent that Gracie could hear the sounds of Burniss' mother working in the kitchen. Maybe Mrs. Watermeister was wondering when Gracie would get down to business and play with Burniss. After all, that was the reason Gracie had given for coming.

The real reason I came, Gracie admitted to herself, is that Lizzie said she wasn't Burniss' friend. I came to make up for that. Gracie was angry with herself for trying to undo Lizzie's rudeness. In desperation, her eyes darted around the room. There were no toys lying about the way there were at home. Even the embroidered cushion on the couch didn't look as though it could be tossed around. Suddenly Gracie said to Burniss, "Sing something else for me."

"Jack . . . Armstrong?" Burniss asked.

Gracie nodded and after a moment, Burniss closed her eyes and began to rock and sing:

> "Wave the flag for Hudson High, boys;
> Show them how we stand.
> E-ver sha-all our team be champions
> Known throughout the land."

Gracie clapped, and Burniss opened her eyes and smiled.

"Burn, that was great!" Gracie said. "How come you never told anybody you were such a good singer?" Burniss smiled and ducked her head.

While they waited for the cake to bake, Gracie and Burniss put on a show for Mrs. Watermeister. Gracie pretended to be the announcer, and Burniss sang all the songs that Gracie could think of from the radio programs.

Later, on her way home, Gracie thought about the gentle safe closeness between Burniss and Mrs. Watermeister. As she walked along, she saw that the vineyards on either side of the road were skeletons of pole and wire and leafless vine. That's how her family seemed now with Crawford in their midst. There was nothing soft or restful about the family anymore. With her hands punched into her pockets, Gracie walked slowly. Her thoughts drifted to Roberta and the episode yesterday afternoon while Mama and Daddy were away. "Hide Crawford. Hide him quick," Roberta had said. Then, in the twinkling of an eye, she had been able to say, silly as you please, "Hold your horses, guys . . ."

That was the way it was going to be with Crawford. All of them were going to be sorry that he was part of the family. They were going to bury him in their midst and then pretend that everything was fine and dandy. When people came, they were going to hide him upstairs and then laugh and have fun downstairs and do things that were important to them and pretend. She was going to do it, too.

The odor of Roberta's permanent greeted Gracie at the door. The kitchen was empty except for Dionne. Gracie crawled under the table to her and sat cross-legged with the cat on her lap. As she smoothed the cat's side, she could feel the scar where King had torn her. The ridge in Dionne's fur brought back that afternoon when she was injured and Uncle Hugh had said to just put her under a bush. Just put her under a bush to die. Just hide her to die was what he meant.

Gracie was still petting Dionne when she heard Roberta call up the stairs from the hall: "Wieners for supper, Ma? If you want, I'll fix them. After all, you spent the afternoon on my hair."

Mama called down, "Some corn relish would be good with wieners. There are some pints of it on the shelf just to the left of the string beans. I'll be down shortly."

Roberta came into the kitchen. Cautiously, Gracie lifted Dionne from her lap and moved so that she could peep out at Roberta's hairdo. "Oh-h!" she exclaimed.

Roberta turned away from the mirror. "Grace Prayther! You have no business spying on me!" She stood with her hands on her hips.

Gracie's face showed her feelings: *Why, I didn't recognize my own sister! I feel sorry for anybody with hair that looks like that! Whatever possessed Roberta to have to have a permanent?*

Roberta suddenly looked as though she were going to cry. Gracie crawled out from under the table. Roberta turned back to the mirror. "It's awful; I hate it," she said, pulling at a little corkscrew of hair on her forehead. "My head looks like a fuzzy mop. It looks like a . . . like a . . . a fur ball!"

"Well, it's not straight as a string like mine," Gracie offered, looking over Roberta's shoulder. She watched as her sister dabbed her eyes.

Roberta began to tilt her head this way and that, trying different faces with her hair. "Do you think it looks natural?" she said to Gracie's reflection.

Gracie's mouth fell open. She searched for words.

Roberta began to giggle. "If you could see your face . . ." she said.

"I can see it, you dodo," Gracie said, sticking her tongue out at herself in the mirror.

"Here," Roberta said, handing her sister the brush, "see what you can do with the top of my hair toward the back there where it sticks up."

Mama came downstairs then and cocked her head to look at Roberta's permanent. "It'll soften after it's washed once or twice. Truth to tell, it's pretty. Makes you look more grown-up, too."

Gracie tried to look at Roberta's hair through Mama's eyes. I suppose I won't mind it once I get used to it, she thought.

15

The day after teachers' institute, the Christmas season officially began at school. Mrs. Coatum passed out pieces to the first-, second-, and third-graders to memorize for the Christmas program. Mrs. Coatum skipped Burniss. Long after the teacher had gone on about something else, Burniss sat waving her hand in the air. Finally, Mrs. Coatum said, "Put your hand down, Burniss."

Gracie looked up from the sentence she was diagramming in her English workbook. Instead of Burniss, she pictured Crawford (when he was bigger) sitting and waving his hand because he wanted to do all the things everyone else did. Gracie could almost hear Mrs. Coatum saying, "Put your hand down, Crawford." With her elbow propped on her desk and her chin in her hand, Gracie frowned at Mrs. Coatum.

After school, Gracie whispered to Nanny Olive, "Did you notice how Mrs. Coatum skipped Burniss — never gave her a piece?"

"Yes, I saw," Nanny Olive said. "You'd think she could at least give her a chance.

"Listen, I have to leave. Grandma's taking me uptown to get blue ribbon. That's all we need to finish what she's helping me make for Crawford. I'm determined to get over to see that baby before we go to Florida. We're leaving Sunday. So long, blood brother."

Once, in Erie, Mama had put a mattress out to air when she was doing her spring cleaning. Roberta and Gracie and the boys next door had been cavorting around on the mattress while Mama stood talking over the fence to the boys' mother. Roberta and the boys had rolled Gracie up in the mattress and wouldn't let her out. She had been smothering and couldn't do a thing about it. That's how she felt now about the news that Nanny Olive would probably ask to come over to see Crawford tomorrow because she had finished his present and wanted to give it to him.

Lizzie fluttered the paper with her Christmas piece written on it in Burniss' face as Burniss was getting ready to go home. "Ha, ha," Lizzie said, "you didn't get a piece."

Burniss snatched the paper and Lizzie sprang at her. Gracie slapped Lizzie. Lizzie grabbed her paper, stuck her tongue out at Gracie and Burniss, and said, "I'm not walking with you two brats — I'm going with Roberta." She flounced out of the school building and ran, crying, "Wait up for me, Roberta!"

As Gracie and Burniss walked along, Gracie was quiet with worry. Somewhere along the line she should have told Nanny Olive about Crawford. She didn't know what she would do. She wouldn't even think about it.

Shaking loose from the thoughts about Crawford and Nanny Olive, she said to Burniss, "It's almost Christmas — you know that?"

Burniss nodded.

"Sing 'Jingle Bells,'" Gracie said. Burniss sang.

"What's this song?" Gracie asked and began to hum "Jolly Old Saint Nicholas."

"Santa Claus," Burniss said. Then she began to sing the song. She knew all the verses.

"Burniss, that's amazing," Gracie said. "How about 'Away in a Manger'? That's a good one."

As Gracie was delivering Burniss to Mrs. Watermeister, a thought spilled out of her before it had even taken shape in her head. She said, "Mrs. Watermeister, Burniss has a solo in the Christmas program at school."

"Oh, my," Mrs. Watermeister said, putting an arm around Burniss. "A part in the program — a solo — isn't that something!"

The lie she had told Mrs. Watermeister, as well as the worry about Nanny Olive's coming to see Crawford, made Gracie feel sick all the way home. She walked slowly so that she wouldn't jiggle her stomach and head too much.

The next morning Gracie still felt "puny," as Mama said when somebody was ailing with something she couldn't just put her finger on. She tried to close her ears to Lizzie's saying her Christmas piece over and over and over again as they walked along Miller Road.

Burniss wasn't feeling up to par this morning, Mrs. Watermeister said, and it was too bad because she was really anxious to go to school. She thought she'd better keep her home, though, because she didn't want to take any chance on her being sick for the program — not with a solo to sing.

Clouds hugged the horizon like wool blankets. The sun was a faded disk behind them. The cold crept into Gracie's bones. Nanny Olive came racing down her driveway, coatless and hatless.

"Gracie!" she cried, "and you too, Lizzie! Come up to the house; come on. I have a surprise. I finished you-know-what. I couldn't wait to show you." Nanny Olive urged them up the drive to the Moores' weather-worn house, and they followed her around to the back door.

"Come on in," Nanny Olive said, running up the steps. She opened the door and tried to push aside a huge black dog. "Go on, Cookie, move," she ordered.

Lizzie began to squeal, and Nanny Olive's grandmother came to the door. "Cookie, if I get me a gad, you'll move. This little girl is afraid of you."

Cookie stood wagging her tail, and old Mrs. Moore said, "Nanette, put her down in the cellar."

"Lizzie, Cookie wouldn't hurt a flea," Nanny Olive said as she tugged the dog away by her collar. Nanny Olive's grandmother reached out her hand to help Lizzie inside. Gracie followed.

"I don't like dogs and I don't like roosters, either," Lizzie said.

Grandma Moore patted her shoulder. "Well, Nanette Olivia is right — that old dog is gentle as can be, but we'd just as soon have her down in the cellar. As for roosters — the place for them is in the stew pot." Nanny Olive's grandmother's eyes twinkled. She was a spry woman in a pink dress and a crisp apron.

"I like drumsticks but I don't like liver," Lizzie volunteered. "Mama said eat it and I did and I throwed up on my blanket and my nighty and my hair and . . ."

The kitchen was so warm. Gracie smoothed her bangs away from her forehead and fumbled with the coat button at her neck. Lizzie blabbed away about throwing up. Nanny Olive's grandmother gave her a little hug and said, "Oh, you're such a one." Nanny Olive, who had come up from the cellar, was laughing at Lizzie, too.

Lizzie began to show off. "Puke," she said.

"Oh, no no no no no, that's not nice." Nanny Olive's grandmother put a finger to Lizzie's lips. Then she said to Nanny Olive, "You run upstairs now and get those booties, or all you youngsters will be late for school."

Nanny Olive ran upstairs. A coal stove was making the kitchen so hot that Gracie's head swam. Grandma Moore was saying, "Nanette is that proud of those booties. Why, she's worked! Usually she's such a helter-skelter — can't sit a minute . . ."

Gracie felt as though she couldn't see out the sides of her eyes. She opened the door and ran out and down Moores' drive. She ran all the rest of the way to school with her chest begging for air and a stitch boring into her side. She peeled off her coat in the cloakroom and jammed her lunch box onto the shelf. Gracie didn't even hear Mrs. Coatum's scolding as she clattered into her seat and put her head in her hands. In a moment, she let her head sink to the circle of darkness her folded arms made against the desk top.

Shortly, she heard Lizzie say from the cloakroom, "In faps, my mother is going to holler at Gracie for not walking me past the Batten Woman's."

"You're okay," Nanny Olive said. "I walked you. Something must be the matter with Gracie."

Now Nanny Olive was standing beside Gracie. Past the edge of her desk, Gracie could see Nanny Olive's shoes. She pressed her head closer against her arms and squeezed her eyes shut.

"Are you sick? How come you ran off like that? You sick?" Nanny Olive stooped on her haunches. Her hand was on Gracie's shoulder, gently begging her.

Gracie prayed fiercely for opening exercises to make Nanny Olive sit down in her seat.

All morning Nanny Olive nagged at her back and her braids. "What's the matter? What'd I do? Look, hey, psst — it's snowing. Aren't you glad?"

There was no answer.

Between fourth-grade history and fifth-grade history, Gracie got out of her seat and walked up to Mrs. Coatum.

"Could I change my seat? Nanny Olive's bothering me."

At first Mrs. Coatum refused to believe what Gracie was saying. Gracie waited. Finally Mrs. Coatum said, "Well, if you want to, you may move your things and sit at the table in the back of the room. I don't know where else you'd sit."

The table at the back of the room was a place with a bad reputation. While Gracie was withdrawing everything from her desk but her and Nanny Olive's soap eraser, her head seemed empty as a shell. The chair legs screeched as she drew the chair away from the table and sat down. Her face flamed. This was what Crawford had made her do. She hated him.

At afternoon's end, Nanny Olive threw the chopped-up pieces of their soap eraser on the table at the back of the room. "Just tell me a reason," she said through clenched teeth.

After school, Gracie dragged through falling snow, following Roberta and Wreath and Lizzie at a distance, taking the long way home to avoid Nanny Olive. A snowball smacked her between the shoulders, and in a strangled voice Nanny Olive cried, "Why are you mad at me?"

Roberta turned and said, "Gracie, you oughta be ashamed. You're a traitor to your best friend." Gracie ran and drove both fists at Roberta.

Frank dodged past her. "What a spitfire," he said and

Gracie drove her fists at him, too. Then she ran past them all.

Snow, like dirty lace curtains, filled the air. Gracie's knee socks were soon wet and raw on her legs. Her face smarted. Snow-melt mixed with tears and nose-run, and she licked at it. When she got home, Crawford's wail somewhere in the house met her at the door.

Instead of going in, she pulled the door shut again. She didn't want Roberta and Lizzie to see her, and they'd be coming along now, so she crossed the yard and skirted the vineyard. By the last post, she leaned her lunch pail and book bag and then crossed the snow-blanketed garden and started climbing the hill. Her feet sank in the mush of snow and leaf. She was blowing when she came out into the orchard on top of the hill, spurting steam from the climb. She headed for the ledge on the bluff above the lake.

The air of the talking spot was thick with snow. If Nanny Olive were here, she'd tell her. She'd tell her and ease the feeling she had about Crawford. "Why are you mad at me?" the wind seemed to cry. Below her, the lake was hidden in the blank snow.

Suddenly, she was immensely frightened. She scrambled out of the talking spot and began to run. She picked a bad place to climb back down the hill. It was steep. Twice she fell and slid, raw cold biting her thighs. She retrieved her book bag and lunch pail and banged snow off them. The aisles between the grape rows were all but blotted out.

She was startled when the door fell open and Daddy stood back to let her in. "Where were you?" he asked.

"We were worried to death." She ducked past him and the rest of the family waiting uneasily at the table and went upstairs to change her clothes.

In the bedroom, she glimpsed the wet ribbons on her braids' ends. Hastily, she pulled them loose, her plaid one and Nanny Olive's yellow one, and smoothed them over the register to dry. Then she hauled on dry clothes and made herself go down to supper.

There was no talk to hide behind. Her coming in late and scaring them all had squelched everything but please pass the peas. Daddy hollered at Lizzie for swinging her legs to and fro under the table while she was eating.

After supper, Roberta washed the dishes, and Gracie dried. She didn't say anything about the potato that Roberta had left stuck to one fork. She just wiped it off on the dishtowel. Afterward, she took Hu and went upstairs with her. She didn't care that Hu watched her cry while she wound up Nanny Olive's ribbon and put it in her keepsake box in her bottom drawer.

By and by, Mama came in with Hu's Dr. Denton's. Gracie knew that the angle of her head would hide tears, but she knew her voice would give her away, so she passed Hu to Mama in silence.

Mama sat on Gracie's bed and stripped Hu. Swiftly, Mama diapered her. Then she took a dollop of Vicks from the blue jar and began to rub Hu's chest and back. Hu squirmed and giggled as the cool green Vicks smell pervaded the room. Mama got Hu into her sleepers and then sat on a minute, holding her on her lap, smoothing day and struggle out of her.

"Roberta says you're on the outs with Nanny Olive," Mama said to Gracie. "Why?"

Gracie shrugged and picked at nothing on her dress as she sat cross-legged on the floor in front of the dresser. "I just am, that's all," she said.

"I'm sorry about it," Mama said.

Gracie nodded.

"You scared us all by coming home so late, with the snow and all. We were afraid something had happened to you. We were worried about you."

There was nothing Gracie could say. Her feelings would not take the shape of words.

Later, Gracie lay in bed next to Dionne. She could tell Mama was careful not to notice the cat when she came in to say good night.

16

Morning sounds had been nibbling at Gracie's sleep for a long time. She didn't want to wake up. She didn't want to go to school. How could she go to school and sit at that hateful table and be unfriends with Nanny Olive? She couldn't. Gracie flopped over onto her stomach and tried to make everything inside of her flat and black so that she would be asleep again.

In his bassinet across the room, Crawford was stirring. Above the noises he was making, Gracie heard the back door slam as Roberta and Lizzie left for school. Maybe she would get away with just lying here. Maybe Mama would tiptoe in to get Crawford, glance at Gracie, and say, "Oh, let the poor thing sleep."

Suddenly Gracie thought of Burniss. She had told Mrs. Watermeister that Burniss was going to sing a solo. Gracie sat up, hot with sweat in the chilly room. The program was at eight o'clock Tuesday evening, and this was Friday. She would have to approach Mrs. Coatum about the solo today. It couldn't wait until Monday — Monday, when Nanny Olive would be well on the way to Florida. Gracie punched her fist into her pillow and got up.

From downstairs Mama called, "Gracie! Hurry now; you're late!"

The more she tried to hurry, the more disorganized Gracie became. Half-dressed, she hopped on one foot, trying to haul a blue knee sock on. She lost her balance and had to grab the end of the bassinet to steady herself. Crawford was lying on his back. She pulled the knee sock up and swam up through her dress. While she fussed with the buttons behind her back, she looked at the baby. His eyes reminded her of Daddy's.

"These dagnab buttons," she said into the bassinet. At the sound of her voice, one corner of Crawford's mouth snicked up. There was a watchful look in his eyes . . . and his mouth curling up like that . . . pooh, he was too little to smile yet . . .

"Gracie!" Mama called.

Gracie bent and drove her feet into her shoes. They were as stiff as boards from the soaking yesterday afternoon. She grabbed her book bag. "So long, you," she whispered to Crawford and ran downstairs.

Mama waited with two slices of toast while Gracie struggled into her coat. "I hope things go better today," Mama said. "I hope you and Nanny Olive make it up. You eat this toast along the way. Lizzie went on ahead with Roberta."

Mama closed the door slowly, waiting, Gracie knew, for a sign that she was all right. Waiting for her to say, Oh, don't worry; things'll be fine between me and Nanny Olive. We just had a little argument — didn't amount to anything.

Gracie turned her back on Mama and ran, kicking up spumes of snow. She was on Miller Road before she remembered the toast in her hand. It made her feel bad to throw it into the snow. It made her feel mean for not eating it after Mama had fixed it, after Mama worried and wanted things to be all right for her.

She walked along Miller Road like something wound up, moving to Burniss' just as always. She accepted Burniss from Mrs. Watermeister. A big black crow lighted in the cap of snow on a grape post and took off again with a rusty caw. Burniss walked twice as slowly with boots on. That was all right, though. That way, they'd be sure not to catch up with Nanny Olive.

When the bell sounded in the clean morning, Gracie and Burniss were neither too far from school nor too close. The door had shut on the last child as Gracie urged Burniss across the schoolyard. The kids had already made a slide, sluicing water from the pump down a little grade at the north end of the building, leaving it to freeze in time for recess. It would be a good slide, reaching from the building's stone steps clear down to where the vineyard began. Last time they had made a slide, there had been a big pile-up at the bottom of it, and Leroy had gotten a goose egg on his forehead.

Mrs. Coatum, one hand on the doorknob, was urging kids past her into the classroom when Gracie held the outside door open for Burniss. Gracie made a business of helping Burniss out of her things, watching Mrs. Coatum out of the corner of her eye. When Mrs. Coatum looked around, Gracie said, "Mrs. Coatum, couldn't Burniss sing a song instead of saying a piece for the program? She can sing really well. She sang 'Away in a Manger' for me on the way home yesterday. I could make sure she practices so that she knows it perfectly." Gracie wished she could say what she had to say in a way that would make Mrs. Coatum stop closing the classroom door and getting right at the opening exercises before they wasted any more time. She straightened up with Burniss' mittens and scarf in her hands.

"Burniss would be better off if you'd let her take care of her own things," Mrs. Coatum said. "Come on now, Burniss, it's time you learned to take care of your own wraps. You're a big girl, much too big for Grace to be waiting on you."

Dutifully, Burniss hung her coat on a hook in the cloakroom and tried to make her hat and mittens and scarf roost on top of it. They coasted to the floor, and Burniss looked down at them.

"Burniss, pick them up. Grace, leave her to figure it out. Get your wraps off and get in here. If you want to make the effort to prepare Burniss with something for the program, you may, but I won't be pleased and neither will the audience if she just stands up there with a finger in her mouth that evening. You see that your own work is complete and then you may take Burniss into the cloakroom to hear her song or whatever you have in mind, if you have extra time."

Gracie edged past Mrs. Coatum, and Mrs. Coatum pulled the door shut, leaving Burniss in the cloakroom. Like the crow homing in on the fence post, Gracie started for her old seat. Then, her cheeks heating with confusion, she had to walk right past Nanny Olive Moore to get back to the table.

Gracie's books, which she had left neatly stacked the afternoon before, were all messed. Someone had played tick-tack-toe on her tablet. Her pencil was gone. While her eyes were shut as she said the Lord's Prayer, wandering along after Mrs. Coatum's certain voice, she remembered the look on Crawford's face — that look in his eyes that tripped a smile. She wondered if Mama knew he could smile.

Later, when Mrs. Coatum was hearing the third-graders read, Gracie went quietly and let Burniss out of the cloakroom. After a glance to see whether Mrs. Coatum was paying any attention, she slipped into the cloakroom and stuffed Burniss' mittens into her coat sleeve. Burniss had managed to hang up the scarf and hat.

At noontime, Gracie was in a pile-up at the bottom of the slide right next to Nanny Olive. "Are you still mad at me?" Nanny Olive whispered down her neck.

Not answering, Gracie rolled out of the tangle of bodies and scrambled to her feet and ran to get in line for another slide. Her turn came up and she backed well beyond the slide's beginning so that she could get a furious running start.

She was already running when Earl yelled, "Out of my way, Prayther!" She didn't intend to give up her turn. Earl had already had more turns than anyone else. She shot onto the ice, twisting sideways, extending her arms on either side so that she would slice through the air. It would be the best slide she'd ever slid.

"Look out!" she called to stragglers at the bottom of the ice. Then Earl's high-tops knocked her off her feet and she fell heavily on her back.

"I told you to get outa the way, you dummy," Earl sang. At least it seemed to Gracie that he sang it, glad he had killed her. And she was dying, she was sure of it.

"Wind's knocked out of her," someone said into her eyes.

Then air tore into her and a groan tore out against her will. Roberta and Wreath were pulling her to her feet. It hurt.

"Are you okay? Are you okay?" Roberta asked. When Gracie didn't answer, Roberta screeched, "Earl Schuster, you dumb-head!"

Suddenly Nanny Olive whirled from the circle of children who were staring at Gracie. She ran at Earl and brought her mittened fists down against his chest. Because his feet were on the slide, he went down. He twisted and grabbed Nanny Olive by the ankle, toppling her over. He scrabbled toward her, shoved her face into the snow, and then rolled her over and plopped snow onto her face.

Gracie pulled her arms free from Wreath and Roberta. If Mrs. Coatum hadn't opened the door, Gracie would have tackled Earl. She would have gotten a stranglehold on him.

Mrs. Coatum, the cloakroom broom in her hand, walked right down into the snow and broomed Earl with the bristles.

"Watch it!" he squawked before he realized what was happening to him and who was doing it. Mrs. Coatum broomed him all the way up the steps and into the cloakroom. "I always get the blame!" he howled.

A minute later the bell rang, and it was fifteen minutes yet until one o'clock.

Lozenges of snow still lay here and there on the cloakroom floor when Gracie and Burniss went out there after Gracie had written the answers to her history questions on a sheet of tablet paper. Gracie arranged two chairs on either side of the wide brown register. She and Burniss sat on two of the chairs and rested their legs on the other two. Burniss was wearing long tan stockings hitched with hose-supporters hung from a pantywaist. Gracie was glad Mama had given up insisting on long stockings. There were still plenty of "ho-supporters," as they called them, floating around in the buffet drawer. The baby announcements that Mama hadn't sent out were in there, too, Gracie remembered. She sighed and Burniss looked over at her.

"Okay, Burn, you've got to sing 'Away in a Manger' to me. Sing. I'll listen and see how you do." Gracie leaned back in the chair and closed her eyes.

Burniss did not start immediately, so Gracie nudged her gently with her elbow, still not opening her eyes. "Sing, Burn. Come on and sing 'Away in a Manger' for me."

She needs to be primed — like a pump, Gracie thought. She sang a little of the song herself, feeling awkward and embarrassed by the way her voice sounded. She opened her eyes. "Sing, Burniss." She smiled at the little girl.

Burniss arched her neck as though something was caught in her throat. Suddenly she began to sing. Gracie nodded encouragement and closed her eyes again to listen. The song gave her a fleeting Christmasy feeling here in the cloakroom, where it was warm and dim and smelled of wet wool. She liked being in here with Burniss. Burniss was like Hu — she was a safe person. You didn't have to worry about her sitting in judgment on you.

What did Nanny Olive think of her? She must think she was the two-facedest person that ever came up the pike. Again, Gracie saw herself going up to Mrs. Coatum and asking to change her seat because Nanny Olive was bothering her. Her cheeks burned. She felt sick — sick of herself — sick of a person who could do that to her best friend. She groaned, and Burniss stopped singing.

Gracie opened her eyes. Burniss was looking at her. "It's okay, Burn; I just had a pain, that's all. You're doing good. Sing some more for me — it'll make my pain better."

Burniss started up again and Gracie closed her eyes over the sting of tears. Waves of feeling about Crawford and what he had made her do hurt so that she moved her hands to grip the sides of the wobbly green chair.

17

Christmas was almost upon them. Mama let Roberta iron the white tablecloth with hemstitching around it so that it would be all set for Christmas Day. They brought the big cardboard box that held all of the Christmas decorations down into the living room. They hung the best wreath in the living room window. The other one was losing its fuzz, so they put that one in the dining room. In the evening when they were listening to the radio, they would turn off all the lights and plug in the wreaths. Lizzie had made a red and green paper chain that stretched all the way across the kitchen. It kept falling down on them, but they kept sticking it together again, standing on a kitchen chair to pinch the loose paper ends until the paste dried enough to hold. Gracie was surprised that Mrs. Coatum hadn't noticed how much paste was disappearing from school. Lizzie had brought home a Vicks jar full of it.

Friday evening as Gracie cut the little cartoon out of the front page of the paper, she said, "There are only five shopping days until Christmas. I'm going upstairs and see how much money I have saved up."

Roberta said, "I know one thing — I don't have very

much money. Nobody'd better expect anything that's costly from me."

"Don't give me checkers," Lizzie said. "You gave me that last year and so did Gracie."

Gracie went upstairs and took the Prince Albert tobacco can that held her money out of her dresser drawer. Crawford, who was lying on his stomach in his bassinet, raised his head a bit. She supposed she'd wakened him. She set the tobacco can on the bed and picked him up, curling the flannel blanket around him. He was getting heavy. She perched on the edge of the bed and held him for a minute, rattling the bank for him. There wasn't any question but what he smiled now.

Saturday afternoon Daddy took them uptown to do their Christmas shopping. He took Lizzie with him and let Roberta and Gracie go to Woolworth's by themselves.

"I don't know why I even bothered to come, I'm so short of money," Roberta said as she and Gracie let themselves into the festooned dime store.

Gracie said, "Well, you shouldn't have bought that permanent so close to Christmas. You should have waited until after you had a chance to earn some money picking cherries this summer. It's your own fault you don't have any money." Gracie was sorry after she'd said it; it didn't help. "I could lend you fifty cents or so." She took the tobacco can out of her pocket.

"You brought that tobacco can!" Roberta cried. "Gracie, you are so embarrassing." Roberta's words dwindled to a whisper. She had spotted someone. Gracie saw Frank paying the clerk for a Miss America bar.

Roberta took the coins from Gracie. "Thanks," she said. "Okay, I owe you seventy-two cents. Don't come around me clinking that tobacco can." Roberta patted her fuzzy hair into place and ducked out of the aisle she and Gracie were in and moved toward the counter where Frank was. "Fancy meeting you here," Gracie heard her say. She wrinkled her nose in disgust.

Gracie wedged her bank into her jacket pocket and strolled up and down the aisles, relishing the smells and sights of the dime store. A Christmas record by Gene Autry was playing somewhere. Gracie lingered in front of the soap erasers in the school-supplies display for a moment and then turned away sorrowfully. It was hard to remember that she and Nanny Olive weren't friends. If things hadn't turned out the way they had, she would have bought a soap eraser and red ribbons for Nanny Olive. Candy too, maybe.

Later, with her shopping finished, Gracie sat on one of the chairs in the front of the store, waiting for Roberta. As she arranged and rearranged the purchases in her shopping bag, a very fat woman, two chairs away, eyed her with a smile.

Suddenly, Roberta appeared beside her. "You're done already!" she squealed. "I haven't even started yet!" Roberta wrung her hands and looked at the big plain clock above them on the wall. "Oh, criminy!"

"You haven't started?" Gracie said. She bent over, tucking the bag down around the Hind's Honey and

Almond Creme that she had bought Mama, because she'd bought Roberta the same thing.

"Frank and me went and had a soda. He treated me. What'll I get for people? What do you want? Oh, crim-iny, this Christmas shopping is so hard and it's so costly." Roberta's eyes roved frantically around the store. "And Daddy'll be here any minute . . ." Suddenly she ordered: "Shut your eyes. Don't look at what counter I go to." She dodged away.

Gracie thought to herself, Now, wouldn't I look stu-pid — sitting here with my eyes shut. She cast a side-long glance, and just as she had suspected, the fat woman was grinning. Gracie bent over her shopping bag.

She had almost bought nail polish for Roberta. She had even had the red bottle in her hand, cold and sharp as a ruby — the nail polish in one hand and her stupid tobacco-can bank in the other. She found she couldn't shake out coins in front of the cosmetic counter. Any-body who kept her money in an old tobacco can was immensely far from being able to buy nail polish grace-fully, or lipstick or rouge or a Toni, or anything that was displayed on the counter in front of her. Like a thief, she slipped the nail polish back into its niche, closing the glossy scarlet ranks and turning tail. Later, after she had shaken all of her money out while she stood in a corner of the toy department and put it in her pocket, she went guiltily back to the cosmetic coun-ter and bought the two little bottles of Hind's Honey and Almond Creme. Even then, she was shamefaced, handing the money over to the clerk.

"Looking for you, by any chance?" the fat woman said, leaning over to pat Gracie's arm and then jerking her thumb toward the door of the dime store, where Daddy stood, looking anxiously for them.

Lizzie was the only one in the car who talked on the way home. She said, "Keep out of my room or I'm telling — and I mean it. And you're not allowed to even go in and get Hu out of her bed. You tell me, and I'll hand her out to you. Don't go in my room for diapers. Or anything. And that's final.

"Daddy, I just bet Gracie's going to snoop for what I got her. Roberta, I bet you wish you had what I got you right this minute. It's pink. I got Hu a ball. But I can play with it just till she gets big enough to catch. But nobody else can play with it. It costed five cents. You want to know what I got Mama?" Lizzie got up on her knees and leaned over the back of the front seat to look at Gracie and Roberta. "You want to know?"

"No," Roberta said.

"Well, that's good, because I'm not telling anyway. I'm not telling what I got anybody. They just have to wait until Christmas. And that's final." She turned around and slid down onto the seat and they drove the rest of the way home in silence.

The kitchen smelled of soup. Its steam fogged the windows. Mama was at the table, cutting biscuits out of a round of dough. Hu sat in the highchair beside her, poking holes in a little wad of dough that Mama had given her. "Looks like Santa Claus marching through here," Mama said to Hu as Gracie and Lizzie went through the kitchen.

"Mama," Roberta said, "next Christmas, I'm going to get better stuff for people." She sighed.

"There's always another Christmas in the offing. We do the best we can," Mama said, trying to make Roberta feel better.

As Gracie closed her bedroom door and began to spread her purchases in a row across the bed, she felt sorry for Roberta — not having a whole bedful of things to admire.

The bag rattled as she freed the chick fountain that she had bought to give to Daddy. As she set it on the bed, she thought about his silence on the way home. He hadn't followed her and Roberta and Lizzie into the house. She imagined that he had spent some of the money from Household Finance and that he was taking the things out of the trunk of the Plymouth to hide them in the garage, building Christmas separate from Mama this year. It was too bad. Christmas put such a burden on people to be joyous and to try to do things for other people. She didn't think Mama could be joyful spending money from Household Finance. It certainly didn't do anything for Roberta's humor to have to spend a borrowed seventy-two cents. Gracie sighed. Christmas was just a big muddle, that's what.

The rubber Mickey Mouse that she had bought for Crawford smiled up at her from the bed. She picked it up, fingering its slim rubber tail and tracing the big buttons on its pants. When she looked at it and at all the presents on her bed, she couldn't help feeling the same way she felt when the wreaths were lit. It was the same feeling she always got when it started to snow just as evening was coming on. Now she wished she had bought the things for Nanny Olive. She could have wrapped them up and put them under the tree at school for the fake Santa Claus to pass out at the Christmas program. No, that wouldn't be any good — Nanny Olive wasn't even going to be at the program.

After a minute, Gracie picked up the Mickey Mouse. I wonder if Crawford will like this, she thought. She tiptoed over to his bed with the mouse behind her back. Crawford's head was turned to the side and he was contentedly sucking his thumb.

"Hey, hey you," she whispered. "I got you something. Look." She lowered the mouse inside the bassinet until it was opposite Crawford's eyes. He sucked his thumb, paying no attention. She lifted him up, shoved the drift of bags off her bed onto the floor, and sat on the edge of the bed with him. He lay looking up at her, his hands balled into little fists just below his chin.

"Lookit," she said. To make him look, she had to hold the mouse right in front of his face. "Boo," she said softly for the mouse. She peeked from behind the toy to see how Crawford liked it. His eyes were round, the same blue as Daddy's. She pranced the mouse up Crawford's stomach toward his chin. He blinked. Then his eyes steadied and his mouth fell open in a crooked smile.

When Roberta yelled for her to come and set the table, Gracie had to plunk Crawford down, scrabble her presents back into their bags, and hide them in her closet. Downstairs, Mama asked her if she'd get Crawford and sit in the rocker to give him his bottle. Lizzie could help Roberta.

The living room was rosy with the light from the wreath. Daddy was lying on the couch. The Christmasy light, Daddy lying there so silent, Crawford on her lap hungrily taking his milk . . . Upstairs, she hadn't even thought about Crawford's having only one foot. Down here, with Daddy lying silently on the couch, that's all she could think of.

18

Trouble had already started at home even before Gracie got back from school the afternoon before the program. She and Burniss had stayed after school for a few minutes to paste pictures of lighted candles on all the windows. The room looked nice, Gracie thought, as she looked around with satisfaction at the red and green swags of paper chain over the window and door frames. Frank had cured the Christmas tree of its list by wiring it to the wainscot. The curtain for the play was in place and at last rehearsal had opened and shut without a hitch. Mrs. Coatum had erased the reindeer "doo" that Earl had chalked underneath the big reindeer he had drawn on the side blackboard. Gracie chuckled inside. Earl had drawn the pile under the reindeer, and everyone had roared with laughter. At first, Mrs. Coatum couldn't figure out what ailed them. Nobody would tell. It was while Gracie and Burniss were pasting the candles on the windows that Mrs. Coatum had finally discovered what Earl had done. With a click of her tongue, she had marched back to erase it.

On the way home, Burniss had been able to sing "Away in a Manger" without the least trouble. Gracie was feeling cheerful as she let herself in at the back door.

Mama was in the kitchen standing at the sink. The prickly smell of Old Dutch Cleanser hung in the air. Lizzie was standing barefoot in a summer dimity dress, crying. Roberta was in the pantry doorway. "I'm not going," she said angrily.

"Lizzie, you can't wear a summer dress in the middle of winter," Mama said, ignoring Roberta.

Gracie walked across to the cellar door and opened it to hang up her coat. She felt as though she were crossing a battlefield.

"Mama, this is my best dress and we're supposed to wear our best dresses tonight," Lizzie said. She stamped her bare foot on the linoleum.

"You're not going to wear a dimity dress in December," Mama said.

Gracie felt sorry for Lizzie, because she couldn't seem to hear the finality in Mama's voice. "Ma-maaa," Lizzie bellowed. A minute later, she stopped crying and said to Mama's back, "I'm wearing it, so there." Then she ran and Mama went right behind her with the dishrag still in her hand.

White-faced, Roberta cried after Mama, "Mama, I'm

not going to the Christmas program if we take that baby along."

In an instant, Mama was back, red spots smoldering on her cheekbones. She took Roberta by the shoulders, dishrag and all. Behind them, in the dining room, Daddy appeared with Hu on his shoulder. He set her down on the table.

"Mama," Roberta said, "do you think I want my friends to see that baby? Do you think I want my friends to see that we have a baby like that?"

Mama said, into Roberta's face, "Roberta, that baby will be wrapped up in a blanket. He'll be . . . he'll be . . ." Her hands dropped from Roberta's shoulders and she turned to lean her forehead against the pantry door-frame. She was crying, but there was no sound to it — only the roll of her shoulders like waves moving shoreward.

Roberta ran, crying aloud, the way she had run once before. Daddy tried to turn Mama away from the door-frame and toward him, but she wouldn't move. Gracie didn't know how she got past them. She picked Hu off the dining room table and went upstairs with her. In Hu and Lizzie's room, Lizzie lay curled up on her bed. All she had on was her slip. Her dimity dress was lying on the floor. Lizzie didn't even look at Gracie as she took diapers and Hu's Dr. Denton's off the end of the crib.

Gracie went into her own room with Hu and closed the door. She let Hu play with her collections, talking to her only when it was necessary. Crawford was growing more and more fussy. Gracie picked him up from the bassinet and held him. He sucked hungrily at his fist but soon turned angrily from it because it wasn't his bottle. He began to cry, and Gracie jiggled him, saying "Sh, sh-sh, sh-sh," over and over again.

The bedroom door opened and Mama came in and took Crawford from Gracie in silence. As she left the room, she said, "None of us is going to school tonight. You may as well get ready for bed." She hurried down the hall and went downstairs with Crawford.

Gracie wanted to run to the railing and yell, Mama! I *have* to go to school. All the rest of you can stay home and fight and be mad if you want to, but I *have* to go to school. *I'm going!*

She didn't say anything. Instead, she sat frozen on the bed. Even when Hu pulled her scrapbook of newspaper pictures of Princess Elizabeth and Princess Margaret Rose down onto the floor and opened it, Gracie didn't move. I don't care if Burniss won't sing, she thought; I don't even care.

Hu pulled a picture out of the scrapbook, tearing it. Without a word, Gracie got up and pushed Hu away from her book. She put the torn picture back into it and put the scrapbook on the table. She tightened the lid on the sodamint bottle of teeth as tight as she could and gave it to Hu. Then she picked her up and carried her in to her crib. Hu lay quietly, holding up the bottle to show Gracie. Gracie nodded and patted Hu's stomach. In a minute, the baby rolled over with the bottle of teeth clutched in her hand, content. Before she left the room, Gracie covered Lizzie. Lizzie kicked out against the blanket in her sleep; then she lay still.

Gracie went into the bathroom and shut the door to wait until Mama came back upstairs with Crawford and tucked him into his basket. She stood behind the door, pulling at her braids with nervousness and biting her lip. As she thought about sneaking off and going to school in the dark by herself, she grew more and more afraid that she wouldn't go. If Burniss won't sing, Gracie said to herself, then she won't. If Mrs. Coatum is aggravated, well, it's just too bad. I can't help it. Let her go ahead and be aggravated. Let Mrs. Watermeister be disappointed and embarrassed. Let Burniss be scared to death standing up there in front of a million people . . .

Gracie heard Mama come up and tuck Crawford into his bed. Then she heard her go down the hall and into her and Daddy's room and shut the door. Her heart slammed in her ears. She had to go to school; that's all there was to it.

She took off her shoes and, holding them in her hand, tiptoed down the hall past the sound of low voices rising and falling in Mama and Daddy's room. She took precious minutes to descend the steps quietly. She let herself out the back door without a sound and pulled into her coat and hood as she ran across the snowy moonlit yard.

Once she was on Miller Road, Gracie slowed, panting, to a walk. The vineyard rows on either side of the road cast shadows of pole and wire and vine. A shrew, black against the pale snow, ran across the road in front of her, and Gracie gave an involuntary "Eek!"

When she got to school, cars were angled into the yard, parked companionably. The schoolhouse windows blazed with light. Gracie made her way through the crowd in the cloakroom, being careful to avoid people she knew. As she found a place alongside the far schoolroom wall, the room seemed a blizzard of color and noise. She saw Mrs. Churchill with Agnes' little red-haired brother. There was a hole in the knee of his tan stocking so that his long underwear showed through. He was as roly-poly as Agnes.

At last Gracie saw Mrs. Watermeister. She was sitting in one of the sixth-grade seats, pulling her gloves back and forth through her hands while she waited for the program to begin.

Shortly, Mrs. Coatum took her place in front of the curtain. When people quieted, she welcomed them to the Miller School Christmas Program. Then she stood aside, and the seventh- and eighth-graders began to sing "Deck the Halls."

When the carol was finished, Wreath began to usher first-, second-, and third-graders into position to say their pieces. The program hesitated when Lizzie's turn came, but only for a moment, and then Leroy Thompson, a miniature yule log in his hand, parted the curtains. Burniss was next.

Gracie jockeyed for a position where she could catch Burniss' eye. There Burniss was, in front of the curtain. She had on a red dress with a white embroidered bolero. Her hair was curled and she had a red ribbon tied in it. Her eyes showed how frightened she was. As silence grew, Gracie crushed even closer, stepping on someone's foot. Stooping, she pushed in front of the benches at the front of the room. "Burniss," she whispered urgently. "Burniss . . . Burn . . ."

At last Burniss looked at her. "Away in a-a man-ger," Gracie mouthed. Her eyes begged Burniss to sing, but Burniss only stared at her. Nearby, Mrs. Coatum stirred with impatience. Gracie sang aloud, nodding her head in time to her own thin music. Midway through the first verse, Burniss began to sing. Her eyes glazed and she rocked back and forth, oblivious of all the people watching. The song was so beautiful that Gracie wanted to cry.

The minute people began applauding, Gracie started to push through the crowd. She had to get outside. She had to get home. As she slipped through the door out into the cold sharp night, someone took her elbow, and her skin prickled with shock.

It was Daddy. He steered her to the Plymouth, parked almost in the road. He helped her in and then went around and got into the car himself.

"The baby cried. When Mama went to him, she couldn't find you." He grunted a little as he looked over his shoulder before swinging the car into the road. "I ought to tan your hide, Gracie. You scared your mother and me half out of our wits."

Gracie's kneecaps jerked up and down and her teeth caught the inside of her cheek.

"With all our worries about the baby, I don't know why you have to add to our trouble," he said, glancing across at her. She turned her face sharply away and looked out the window. He went on: "Things are in a turmoil at our house. We're heartsick, all of us. It doesn't make things any easier when you do a silly thing like running off by yourself in the dark."

Gracie stared out the window. She opened her eyes as far as they would go to make room for the tears in them so that they wouldn't spill out and run down her cheeks. She didn't think he was fair to holler at her.

Daddy was so silent as they turned the corner and drove along Freeport that she turned her head just far enough to look at him. He was gripping the steering wheel, and in the moonlight she could see that his jaws were clenched in a terrible sadness.

"I had to go to school tonight on account of Burniss, Dad. Mrs. Coatum didn't want her to be in the Christmas program and Burniss wanted to be in it. I found out she can sing even if she can't say a piece. I asked Mrs. Coatum if it was okay if Burniss sang a solo. The only trouble is — sometimes she won't sing unless I get her started." Gracie's voice petered out. She gave a long sniff to stall the nose-run.

Daddy reached over and patted her arm. He swung the car into their drive.

"Did she do all right?" he asked. "Did she sing?"

Gracie nodded, not trusting herself to speak.

"Look," Daddy said, urging her to look in their kitchen window. "Look — what do you bet Mama's making us some cocoa?"

19

They had gotten through Christmas.

Curiously, Daddy had given Gracie the same thing she gave him — a chick fountain. Gracie tested it in the bathtub on Christmas morning. She filled the Mason jar with water, screwed the little metal saucer in place, and then inverted the jar in the tub. It was surprising that the water didn't overflow the saucer into the tub, emptying the jar. Only enough water flowed into the saucer to fill it. The rest of the water stayed up in the jar. Gracie dumped the water and wiped the jar out with a towel. Spring and baby chickens were a long way down the line.

Mama had knitted a blue sweater for Crawford with a hat to match and she'd made him some new nighties. He had already outgrown some of the things that Hu wore when she was far older than four weeks. Hu claimed all the little rubber and celluloid toys that Santa Claus left. She liked them better than the table and chair set he had brought her. Gracie wouldn't let her keep the Mickey Mouse. "No, this is the baby's," she said. She tied it to the hood of the buggy with a Christmas ribbon so that Hulene couldn't get it loose.

Wednesday evening after Christmas, Gracie barricaded herself in one corner of the playroom. She had a handful of hard candy in her pocket and she wanted to eat it in peace while she read *The Farm Journal* and the chicken catalog Daddy had gotten at Gordon's Feed and Fuel. Roberta was upstairs reading *Under the Lilacs.*

Crawford was crying in the buggy, and Mama was greasing Lizzie's chest and back with Vicks. Lizzie was howling to beat the band. Daddy was already late for the evening shift at G.E. when the phone rang. "Robert, could you get that?" Mama called.

By the time Daddy was finished on the phone, Mama was at the stove, trying to get Crawford's bottle ready.

"That was Hugh," Daddy said, putting on his coat. "He said they had intended to get over to see us Christmas Day but Nita's family came in unexpectedly from Detroit. He says duty calls though, and he and Nita and the boys want to stop by Sunday with some things for the kids."

"I've never been able to find it in my heart to care very much for Hugh," Mama said coldly.

Daddy left in silence, pulling the door sharply to behind him.

Hulene caved in Gracie's barricade of glider pillows. "Uh, uh, uhh," she whined, pointing at Gracie's mouth.

"You can't eat this candy; you'd choke," Gracie said. "Go play. Let me be."

Hu's mouth quivered. Gracie looked at her with her nose running down over her lip, sighed, and got up to go and get a handkerchief. Hu fought against having her nose wiped, and Gracie would have liked to wish her off on Mama. Mama seemed out of sorts, though, so she took Hulene into the living room and held her up to look at the tree lights. Hu picked an icicle off the tree. Gracie took it and draped it over the baby's ear. "Oh, pretty Hu," she said. "Go show Lizzie. She'll think you're a Christmas tree."

"No," Hu said, pulling the icicle off her ear and throwing it down on the floor.

"Gracie, cut out my cutouts for me," Lizzie whined from the couch. She was stuffy and feverish with her cold.

Between Wednesday and Sunday, Gracie could see Mama wind tighter and tighter. Gracie had often heard Mama say that Hugh and Nita rubbed her the wrong way. Gracie sympathized with Mama. She didn't see how Daddy and Uncle Hugh could be brothers, they were so different. Daddy was a quiet person and Uncle Hugh was a big blowhoots.

Sunday morning, Daddy brought a gallon of grape juice up from the cellar and put it in the Frigidaire. "Will that go all right, Bess?" he asked Mama.

"I suppose so," Mama said. She was worried about Crawford. He had caught Lizzie and Hulene's cold, and his crying was high and fretful.

"I wish they weren't coming," Mama said.

Daddy stood uncertainly by the sink. "Well, do you think I should call them? Tell them the kids have colds?" he asked.

"No, I don't," Mama said.

Daddy retreated from the kitchen.

Roberta was leaning on her elbows at the kitchen table, twiddling her curls with her fingers and reading the *Grange Cookbook*. "Here," she said, "here. Ma, can Gracie and I make peanut butter cookies? I promise we'll clean up the mess. We can have cookies with the grape juice when Uncle Hugh and them come."

Mama was pacing the floor, rubbing Crawford's back, taking his temperature with her cheek against his head. "This baby is sicker than I want a baby to be," she said.

Roberta slid away from the table and went into the pantry. Neither she nor Mama was listening to one another. She brought out the flour and sugar canisters and said, "Gracie, get the butter and get out two eggs and we need the peanut butter. These are the kind of cookies you make a crisscross on with a fork, remember?"

Mama went upstairs and Gracie doubted whether she had even noticed that Roberta was planning on baking, because she hadn't turned on the oven. Gracie and Roberta had never turned on the oven by themselves because the gas knob was broken and you had to turn the shaft with the pliers so that the little hole in it pointed straight up. While you were doing that, you had to apply a lighted match to the burner under the oven. It was scary when the ring of gas whooshed to life.

Gracie began to mash the butter. "Who's going to light the oven?" she asked.

"Me, that's who," Roberta said.

She opened all the doors to the range. Then she planted her feet as far back from the stove as she could and still reach the gas knob with the pliers. She held a match aloft in her left hand.

"You know you have to light the match," Gracie said, making a trail down over the slippery butter with the bowl of the spoon.

"I know what I'm doing," Roberta said. She turned the shaft and Gracie smelled the evil gas smell. Roberta couldn't get the match to light by striking it with her left hand.

"Turn off the gas, quick; turn it off!" Gracie said.

Roberta knelt and struck the match across a rough spot on the door of the oven. There was a loud pop and flame spurted from Roberta's fingers and leaped into the stove. Roberta tumbled back.

Gracie's hands flew to her head. "You crazy nut!" she cried. The smell of singed hair hung in the room and when Gracie looked at Roberta, she saw little frizzled gray hairs at her forehead. "My gosh, you could have gotten burned to a crisp!" Gracie told her.

Roberta jumped up to look in the kitchen mirror. "Is my hair wrecked?" she said, peering at herself. "Oh, it's not bad. For crimast sakes, what's lighting a little gas stove? We can't all be ninny babies around here."

They had two pans of cookies cooling on the table, minus the several they had eaten, and a wad of uneven dough lying in the bottom of the mixing bowl when Uncle Hugh's Buick rolled up the driveway.

"Ohmigosh, they're here already," Roberta said. "You want to finish up? I'm sick of this. I've got to go see what I can do with my burned hair." She took flight.

Gracie's hands were greasy and caked with dough. There was flour all over the table and even some on the floor. Through the window, she could see Aunt Nita and Uncle Hugh and Buddy and Junior getting out of the car. Aunt Nita had a shopping bag of Christmas packages.

Behind Gracie, the house was silent. She couldn't decide whether to go and call Mama and Daddy, or whether to wash her hands first, or what. They were already at the back door. The knob turned and Uncle Hugh's ruddy face looked around the corner.

"Well, well, well, who have we here? Is it little Mabel?" he said, leading his family in. "Flour on your snoot," he said, flicking a finger on the end of Gracie's nose. She turned her head and wiped her nose on the back of her wrist.

"Yumm," Uncle Hugh said, taking a cookie and passing one to Aunt Nita. The boys roughhoused over and helped themselves. "Say, where's that brother of mine hiding out, Gracie?" Uncle Hugh asked. Without waiting for an answer, he walked past into the dining room, calling, "Robert?"

As Aunt Nita removed her hat, she discovered that she'd lost an earring. "Bud, Junior," she said, "run out to the car and check for my earring.

"And check on the driveway for it, too," she called after them.

As she began taking packages out of the shopping bag and laying them on the table, Aunt Nita said, "That's the worst thing about earrings. Well, no, that's not the worst thing. The worst thing is to get a pair that pinch. Now, if you could lose both earrings at once, it wouldn't be so bad. To lose just one, though . . . That's a pet peeve of mine — to have just one earring lying around. I can't bring myself to throw it away, because I always have hopes of finding the other one, you know what I mean?"

Gracie had a hard time listening to what Aunt Nita was saying.

Aunt Nita tried to interest her in the packages. "Now I hope I picked right. You know I'm used to buying for boys. I was fuzzy about sizes but . . . Mother busy with the baby?"

Gracie nodded, rolling a wad of dough into a ball in her hands.

"Isn't it too bad about the baby?"

Gracie lowered her eyes.

"We don't know why these things happen, but they do. I guess there just have to be people in the world like that. It's a shame, but that's the way it is. Mother Nature doesn't often go astray, but occasionally . . ." Aunt Nita sighed.

Gracie pinched a piece off the ball of dough because she had decided that it was too large for one cookie.

"I know one thing," Aunt Nita said. "Hugh said he'd never seen his brother so broken up about anything — when he was told about the baby's condition, I mean. Hugh said he just went all to pieces — took it awful hard."

Gracie deposited the ball of dough on the cookie sheet and cut it to ribbons with the fork. Then she scraped it off and balled it up again.

Aunt Nita went to the window. "Those two roustabouts aren't looking for my earring." She rapped on the windowpane and yelled, "Are you looking for that earring? Get off the car!" She turned back to Gracie and, after a bit, said, "I suppose I should thank the Lord that my boys have two sound feet. I oughtn't stand here hollering my fool head off at them."

Gracie took the bowl and scraped the rest of the dough into the garbage can. She heard Mama coming downstairs.

When Mama came into the kitchen, she was carrying Crawford. Worry over him made her greeting to Aunt Nita flat. Aunt Nita busied herself opening some of the packages on the table and holding the things up for Mama to inspect.

Buddy and Junior had come back inside without the earring. They were staring solemnly at Crawford, trying to see where he began and where he left off. Gracie had gotten out the dustpan and broom to sweep up the spilled flour. Dionne jumped out of the pantry and tackled the broom. Gracie knelt for a minute and petted her.

After she had wiped off the table, Gracie lined up a row of glasses and took the gallon of grape juice out of the Frigidaire. Her eye measured the purple fall into the glasses. Crawford was wheezing on Mama's lap as she sat at the head of the table, kitty-corner from Aunt Nita. The boys hung on the back of Aunt Nita's chair, staring at Crawford.

Aunt Nita reached over and tucked the blanket closer around Crawford's legs. She clicked her tongue and wagged her head sorrowfully. Buddy's elbow must have dug into her shoulder, because she said, "Boys, give Gracie some help there. Gracie, they have two good feet; let them carry the drinks in to the men."

Buddy and Junior each took a glass of grape juice and started through the pantry toward the living room. Dionne bounced into the room and hid under the table.

"You know, Bess," Aunt Nita said, "I was put out when Robert didn't bring Hulene out to us when you were in the hospital. We love Huie . . ."

"He was distracted, Nita."

Suddenly Mama gasped. Gracie looked up sharply and saw her looking at Crawford with alarm. He was curled forward on her lap with his chin on his chest and his arms thrown out in a stiff semicircle. He was making the funniest noise in his throat.

Mama was on her feet, crying out, "Robert! Robert! Come quick! Something's the matter with the baby!"

Mama had rushed to the sink and turned on the water. She was trying to strip clothing from Crawford, all the while moaning, "Oh, oh, oh . . ."

After long seconds, Daddy appeared in the doorway, Uncle Hugh behind him. Mama cried, "Robert, he's having a convulsion! We have to get him into warm water!"

"Bessie," Daddy whispered, staring at Crawford, half-naked now in Mama's hands.

Buddy and Junior had come up behind Uncle Hugh and were peering around him at Crawford. Gracie ran over to Mama and Daddy as though to shield them and Crawford from the boys' stares. Then she saw how sick the baby was.

Gracie backed away in horror. She turned and ran to Uncle Hugh, almost driving him into the dining room. "Do something; can't you please do something!"

she begged. Before he could answer, she had dashed around the kitchen table to Aunt Nita, still seated in her chair. "What can we do?" Gracie cried, wringing her hands. "Please get the doctor. Take Crawford to the hospital. Can't we *do* something!"

Aunt Nita and Uncle Hugh seemed to be frozen. Gracie stood in the center of the kitchen and with blazing eyes cried, "Oh, you don't *care!* Nobody *cares!* Nobody *cares* if Crawford dies!" Then, crying desperately, she stooped beside Dionne and, as though they were the only ones in the room, she traced along the little cat's back again and again with one finger. When Aunt Nita and Uncle Hugh came to her, she picked Dionne up and buried her face against her and went on crying.

A long time later, Daddy was the one who came to say good night to her. He sat on the edge of the bed.

"Will Crawford be all right, do you think?" Gracie asked him.

"The doctor said so. His fever is down. The doctor said his fever's being so high was what made him have the convulsion. He's asleep."

"I don't hear him breathing." She raised up on one elbow to try to see the bassinet across the room.

"Mama and I have him in our room. He's not breathing loud the way he was. He's breathing sweet as a kitten now — just the way a young man should."

Gracie let herself back down on the pillow. Daddy sat on in silence, his hand resting on her kneecap. Crawford was all right. That was good.

"Dad?"

His fingers tightened a little on her knee so that she knew he was listening.

"Sorry I screamed at Uncle Hugh and them."

"My God, Gracie, it's time somebody screamed at all of us." He rested his elbows on his own knees and held his head in his hands.

By and by, Gracie said, "Dad? I read an article in *The Farm Journal* that says how important it is to keep records when you're in business. When we get the chickens, I'm going to keep a notebook on just how much we spend. You think that would be a good idea?"

20

The chicks were starting to get their pinfeathers. Every day after school, Gracie would lug Hu's highchair out to the garage and take Crawford out there to watch while she put fresh water in the chickens' fountains and added to the mash in their feeders. She had to take diapers knotted together to tie Crawford in the chair so he wouldn't fall out. At five months, if he wasn't tethered, he'd try to swarm up onto the tray.

Gracie reached into the raised enclosure that she and Daddy had made with hardware cloth and lifted up a chick. It looked so dressed up, with its tiny fans of wing feathers. She set it on the highchair tray, and Crawford tried to grab it. "No, no," she said to him, "it's little; you've got to be tender to it. Here." She caught the chick and held it in her hand. With her other hand, she took Crawford's hand and lowered it over the chick. "Feel how soft?" she said to him. Crawford was still for a second, and then he kicked his legs and spit with glee. Gracie lowered the chick back into the pen and it scurried off. Half the flock ran after it, their toes pattering like sleet on the newspaper spread over the heavy screening that served as the floor of their pen. The garage was tinny with the sound of their peeps.

Crawford reached his arms up to her and she untied him and took him out of the chair so that she could hold him closer to the chicks. Their activity made him squirm, eager to get his hands on them. He wouldn't be content with watching them this afternoon, so she took him out for a walk.

All last fall's snarl had been pruned away from the grape vines and burned. Two wands on either side of the grape stalk were laid along the wire, upper and lower, and tied in place with soft brown twine. Mrs. Watermeister had tied the Praythers' grapes this spring. Burniss came home from school with Lizzie and Gracie each afternoon, and she and Lizzie played together while Mrs. Watermeister finished up. The furrows of plowed earth turned up on either side of the grape rows looked good enough to eat. Gracie showed Crawford the grape leaf buds coming out. They were pink and spring-green and looked good enough to eat, too.

After she had walked a couple of grape rows, Gracie took Crawford to the swing at the end of the front yard and sat with him. Overhead, the cherry blossoms hung like white crocheting. She leaned into spring, woozy with the restfulness of it.

Suddenly Roberta yelled from the front steps, "Hey, how come you get to do nothing but play with Crawford, and I get stuck with all the work! I'll gladly sit on the swing with him and you get in here and set the table!"

"Ah, go chase your grandmother," Gracie yelled back. She took a firm grip around Crawford's waist, jabbed her toe into the dirt, and began to swing. "Hang on, Crawford," she said. The swing wobbled crazily, because she was holding only one rope. The baby liked it. He flapped his arms and legs and laughed.

"Grace Prayther, get yourself in here!" Roberta cried.

Gracie and Nanny Olive had gotten very good at being enemies. They tagged each other for spite in Come Across the Chinese Border or Andy, Andy Over. Each one tried to outjump the other at jump rope, until the enders would yell, "Nanny Olive, get out — give somebody else a chance," or "Gracie, your turn's up. You're hogging the whole recess!"

When Gracie walked down the aisle, she jogged Nanny Olive's desk on purpose — if Nanny Olive hadn't managed to trip her first.

Gracie found that she could live that way, but sometimes when she least expected it, she would find herself wishing that she and Nanny Olive were friends again. She wished they were.

*

Nanny Olive was standing at the board putting up some work for Mrs. Coatum. Gracie was slumped in her chair back at the table. Afternoon sun lit the room. Sweaters lay on the floor or on seats like so many shed skins. Gracie had rolled her knee socks into green doughnuts around her ankles. She stuck her pencil behind her ear, stretched out her legs, and rested.

Up front, Leroy droned through the dullest story ever written. Mrs. Coatum sat listening, half-asleep. Idly, Gracie watched Nanny Olive writing on the board. She liked the way Nanny Olive always made her *t*'s on the end of words. Nanny Olive was wearing her favorite blue dress — the one with piping on the collar, the one that Grandma Moore had patched where Nanny Olive tore it on a grape post. You'd never know it had been torn. Gracie was searching for the mended place when she saw the spot of blood on the back of Nanny Olive's skirt.

Gracie sat up, alert. The cross of blood in the night came back to her. The same thing that had happened to Roberta had happened to Nanny Olive. Gracie saw Earl turn sideways in his seat and prop his feet on Leroy's empty bench. Earl looked bored. He looked ready to finish the afternoon with any kind of mischief he could find.

Before she had time to think, Gracie was on her feet. She moved with studied casualness across the back of the room and turned into the end aisle. She remembered how you lean when you whisper in your best friend's ear.

"There's blood on the back of your skirt."

"Oh, no." Nanny Olive's hand flew to her mouth.

"Go in the bathroom," Gracie whispered. "Leave the door unhooked. I'll get some water and help you to wash it out."

"You're a lifesaver."

Gracie went back to her chair and slouched into it. Nanny Olive, with an odd sideways gait, walked around the back of the room and up the other side to the girls' bathroom door. She let herself in and pulled the door to behind her.

Gracie bided time anxiously and then got out of her chair and walked around and up the end aisle close to the blackboard where Nanny Olive had been writing. When she had her hand on the cloakroom doorknob, Mrs. Coatum looked up suspiciously.

"Grace . . ."

"I was just going to get a drink. My throat's so dry I can't do my geography," Gracie pleaded.

Mrs. Coatum's eyes were reluctant, but she nodded her head and let Gracie go.

When she came back into the cloakroom with her cup full of water from the pump, Gracie listened at the door's crack for a minute. Earl was on his feet sassing Mrs. Coatum. He wanted to go out for a drink, too. For once, Earl is going to be a help to me, thought Gracie, but he doesn't know it. Mrs. Coatum will be too busy paying attention to him to notice me.

Gracie sidled through the door and walked across behind Mrs. Coatum's desk. She had the cup of water in her hand and held it straight down by her side. She walked swiftly, leaving a trail of little drops, and let herself into the girls' bathroom.

Nanny Olive was standing there with her skirt skewed around so that she could see the spot of blood. "Oh, if Earl had noticed . . ." she groaned.

Gracie hooked the door and turned to look at Nanny Olive's skirt.

"You know what it is, don't you?" Nanny Olive asked with some uncertainty.

Gracie nodded. "It happened to Roberta," she said, "back in December."

Nanny Olive said, "The first time it happened to me was when we were in Florida. I wanted to tell you when we came back . . . but . . . you know . . ." Nanny Olive's face was quiet and sorrowful.

"It hasn't happened to me yet," Gracie confided," but Mama thinks maybe it will, soon."

"Maybe it will," Nanny Olive said, holding her skirt out over the toilet so that Gracie could pour water over the stain. "Isn't it a queer odd thing? Is the stain coming out, do you think?"

"Pretty much," Gracie said. She and Nanny Olive stayed in the bathroom all through recess, flapping Nanny Olive's skirt to dry it.

In bed that night Gracie lay at peace, cherishing the tag end of the afternoon. She and Nanny Olive had walked home together, high silliness sweeping them the way spring was sweeping the vineyards.

The next afternoon Gracie took Crawford outside.

She hadn't intended to go all the way to the ledge above the lake with him. She had planned to go only as far as the hill out back to see if there were any dog-toothed violets in bloom. Once she got that far, though, she thought she'd climb up the hill and take a look out over the lake.

The orchard on top of the hill was lit with cherry blossoms. She began to feel excitement as she approached the bluff. This was going to be Crawford's first look at the lake. She turned him with his back against her, facing outward, so that he'd see the whole expanse spread out before him.

"There it is, Crawford. Lake Erie. See how big it is! What do you think, huh?" She liked the stillness of him while he looked.

She picked her way down to the ledge with him and settled with the bluff at her back. It felt so comfortable to be here in her and Nanny Olive's spot. She propped Crawford against her knees to talk to him. It was so warm that soon she took off his flannel nighty so that he wore only his undershirt and diaper. "Hold still," she said while she made a curl along the top of his head with his sweat-dampened hair.

Suddenly, from above, Nanny Olive said, "I knew you'd be here today; I just knew it."

The sounds of Nanny Olive's descent made Gracie want to cover Crawford's legs with his nighty. Instead, she sat holding him and let Nanny Olive sink down on her knees beside them. Crawford, his fist in his mouth, stared at Nanny Olive in surprise.

"Hi," she said to him.

After a moment Gracie said, "Meet my brother — Crawford Charles Prayther."

"Hi," Nanny Olive said again, touching Crawford's fist with a careful finger. He took her finger and tried to chew it. Nanny Olive grinned at him. "Do you bite?" she said. "Do I get to hold him?" she asked Gracie.

"If you want."

Nanny Olive settled beside Gracie, and Gracie passed Crawford to her and helped her to get him adjusted. His curl got mussed in the process and Gracie redid it. "He's going to have curls like Lizzie," she said. Then she stretched out on her side, propping with her elbow and resting her head on her hand. She felt very tired and found she was glad to share Crawford with Nanny Olive. They seemed to like one another.

After a while Nanny Olive said, "The booties... that wasn't a very good present, was it?"

Gracie said, "You didn't know. I didn't tell you. I wanted to, but I couldn't. I was a lot sad about Crawford at first — our whole family was. Now, he's the cock of the walk. I bet Roberta's home bellyaching to Mama because I took him out and she wanted to."

"He's a nice baby," Nanny Olive said, tickling his knee with the end of her braid.

"I know it — I wouldn't trade him."